166 Palms

- a - literary - anthology -

2018

CONTENTS

PREFACE

Change drives the universe, and by extension, our lives and relationships. The Stanford writers featured in this edition of *166 Palms* give voice to tumultuous lives of characters who fear, desire, struggle, deny and flee toward an unsettled destiny. These writers draw us inside their characters' worlds and provide insights to their singular truths.

We are grateful in these uncertain times for the privilege to read work that reminds us what it is to be human.

– Linda Moore
Guest Editor

FOREWORD

Beloved and memorable, the one hundred and sixty-six Canary Island date palms that welcome students and visitors to Stanford University are perhaps the most iconic of the four hundred species and over twenty-thousand individual trees growing on campus. Imagine for a moment that these *Phoenix canariensis* symbolize the bringing together of diverse and gifted learners united in the pursuit of inspiration and discovery. Could it be this indelible spirit then influenced the development of Stanford University's unique novel-writing program where prestigious Stegner Fellows carefully select and mentor aspiring writers from all over the world? Embrace the possibility and discover an anthology inspired by these very ideals, an anthology celebrating the unique voices of extraordinary writers, an anthology appropriately titled, *166 Palms*.

— James Burnham
Managing Editor

THE BLUE VEINS OF YOUR HANDS

-Chapter 4-

Maryam Soltani

"I won't give up love, youth's beauty and wine." - Hafez

"Is it blue?" Marjaneh asked.

"Yeah," Roya answered, disappointed.

"The sea!" Marjaneh screamed. "Is it the sea?"

They were playing "twenty questions" in the back seat of the car, and Marjaneh won again. She often guessed the correct answer before they reached the tenth or twelfth question. Roya looked out the window. The narrow, winding road to the Caspian Sea slithered through arrays of trees. Drops of light drizzled and the whiff of the moist soil sneaked in through the cracked windows. Baba was driving and Mamon, in the passenger seat, kept rewinding and fast-forwarding a cassette tape, looking for a song.

"Found it," she said.

"Thank God," Baba said.

Roya turned to Marjaneh. "I'm tired now. I want to take a nap."

"You hate to lose."

Sattar's singing filled the car. "Booye Mohat zire baroon – the scent of your hair under the rain …"

Roya did hate to lose, but that wasn't the reason she didn't want to play anymore. She yearned to shut her eyes, listen to the music, and dream of Milan.

"Ragaye aabie dastat – the blue veins of your hands …"

She imagined Milan's hands. Thinking about him was by far the best feeling in the world. The bottom of her stomach tickled and her whole body slid into joy, every time she closed her eyes and pictured him.

Traveling north to the Caspian, in summer, was a ritual in her family and Marjaneh always tagged along. This year, though, things were different. Roya had told Milan about the trip, and he and Sepehr decided to go, too.

"Maybe somehow we can all get together and go swimming," Sepehr had said last week.

"But, how?" asked Roya.

"I'll figure something out."

Mamon and Sepehr's mother were old friends. His mother

had told Mamon that Sepehr would be up north, too, but Mamon didn't know anything about Milan. She didn't even know him. Milan was a friend of Sepehr.

"Such a pleasant surprise that Sepehr will be there," Mamon said, turning to Roya and Marjaneh in the back seat. "I gave his mother the address where we'll be staying."

Roya tried to imagine swimming beside Milan, to picture his half-bare body, but couldn't bring the image into focus. Since the 1979 revolution, five years ago, when she was only twelve, men and women weren't allowed on the same beaches anymore, even if they were family members. It was sinful, and punishable, but no one followed the rules. Everybody just found different ways around it and did it privately. There were some fishermen and locals who rented their boats to swimmers. People would ride them to the middle of the sea, far from the beaches, and swim there.

Roya recalled the lively Caspian beaches before the revolution, men and women in bathing suits, tanning or swimming side by side, and the night life: restaurants, discos, shows and concerts. She was nine when she went to her first show, in a beachside restaurant. Googoosh, one of Mamon's favorite singers, had performed. Mamon wore a white summer dress. Her dark hair spilled over her bare shoulders, and her olive skin was tanned evenly except for the pale lines left by the straps of her swimsuit. For some reason Mamon's gold espadrille wedges drew a vivid shape in her mind, with their straw straps that zigzagged up her calves to carefully-tied bows below her knees. Baba wore a light blue shirt. He sipped on a glass of beer and, with his other hand,

13

caressed Mamon's shoulder.

The three of them had danced all night. How happy she had been. She vaguely recalled dozing away on her chair at the end of the night, and Baba carrying her to their villa, the one they often rented. Her memories lingered, but that whole world had been razed. None of those musicians performed or even lived in Iran anymore.

"Yade baroon o tane e tow – the memory of the rain and your body …"

"I can't wait to go swimming with the boys." Marjaneh's whisper penetrated Roya's reminiscences and Sattar's voice. She could smell the fresh cucumber Marjaneh was munching. She opened her eyes. Knitting her eyebrows, she placed her index finger to her nose, and shushed Marjaneh.

The idea of swimming with Milan was thrilling, and despite all the danger she was willing to take the risk. She just had to find a way to hide it from Mamon and Baba. They would never allow it.

The summer heat felt good on her bare skin, as if the humid air was stroking her with warm and soothing oil. She adjusted the straps of her one-piece turquoise bathing suit to move them away from her scars, which, even after a few months, were still tender when touched by her clothing. Over her swimsuit she pulled on a pair of jeans. Her jeans always felt heavier up north because of the humidity, and stuck to her legs. She wore her long robe, placed a cotton scarf on her head and made sure no hair was exposed.

Marjaneh was ready long before she was. She even had her scarf on, which only covered half her head. Lying face up on the bed, she read Forough Farrokhzad's poetry book, "The Sin." Her feet had crumpled the sky blue bed sheet.

They were in the smaller room of the two-bedroom villa Baba had rented for the week. The window above the bed was wide open, allowing the aroma of the sea to seep in and linger.

"Does my Mamon know you brought that?" Roya whispered, pointing to the book.

"Why would I tell her? Does she know we're going swimming with Milan and Sepehr? Which one is worse, reading a banned book or swimming with the boys?"

"Who knows...I hope you're covering your hair better when we get out. We don't want anybody to notice us," Roya said as she ironed out, with her palms, a small piece of paper. The night before, when Sepehr came to dinner, he'd slipped it into her pocket.

"Read it one more time," Marjaneh said, ignoring Roya's comment.

"After the White Plage, you'll pass a big pink villa, the last house you'll see, and we will be there. It's a secluded beach, so no worries. I'll rent a motorboat. Be there at sunset."

Roya read it before tearing the paper into small pieces. She had been to White Plage many times, but never had gone further. Marjaneh got up, hid her book under the mattress and fixed her head scarf. "I'll grab a towel," she said.

The smell of the freshly cut grass and olive trees fused with the breeze that emerged from the sea and stroked Roya's face as she stepped out. With every step she took, she felt her heartbeat in her mouth. They told Mamon they were going for a long walk on the beach, and that they would grab dinner at Freydon's Kabobi and be home before it was too late. Lie after lie after lie. This was all new for her. She had never lied to Mamon. Slowly, she was learning.

The White Plage was crowded. A couple of beach vendors were selling barbeque corn on the cob, and when Roya and Marjaneh passed by one of them, an older man called on them: "Two special ones for two special ladies." He yelled, smiling, displaying missing teeth. With his wrinkled, skinny hands he dipped two ears of corn, already barbequed, inside a huge pot of salt water. "The best on the beach," he continued. Roya ignored him, pretended to be wiping sand off of her plastic flip-flops. Marjaneh laughed. "Not now. We'll be back later," she said.

"Do you have to talk to everybody?" Roya asked, examining her surroundings.

"I'm much friendlier than you are."

"Please don't be. At least, not now."

After they passed the White Plage, the beach became less and less crowded until there was almost nobody around. Marjaneh pointed to a beautiful pink villa ahead of them, facing the sea. In the far distance Roya recognized the boys. Milan had the bottom of his pants rolled up to his knees. His feet sank into the sand and the waves enveloped his ankles. His loose, short-sleeved shirt puffed in the breeze as he bent into the small wooden boat, his hands rummaging for something. Sepehr stood in the water, tall and lean, with that perfect skin, and stared at his friend while

16

fiddling with the handle of the little outboard engine. He seemed lost in his thoughts.

Roya looked around the deserted beach to make sure no one was watching, and then waved to get Sepehr's attention. Out of nowhere two teenaged boys, thirteen or fourteen, appeared and marched by Roya and Marjaneh. One of them made a remark that Roya didn't hear well. Something about two girls walking on the beach without men means sending an invitation for sex, and then they laughed. Roya, trying to ignore them, pulled her scarf further down her forehead.

"Shut up, you idiots," Marjaneh roared at them. "Khar o madar nadarid – don't you have mothers and sisters? I'll go find your mothers and tell them."

Fear in their faces, the boys sprinted away.

Sepehr turned around as if he had felt Roya's waving arm slicing the air, or perhaps he heard Marjaneh yelling. He too inspected the beach to make sure no one was there, and then nudged Milan, or was it more like squeezing his shoulder? Milan heaved upright, saw the girls, and smiled.

Nobody was there, just the four of them in the tiny boat, moving farther away from the beaches that gradually vanished. The sun slowly sank into the water, leaving behind layer after layer of orange and yellow in the sky.

Roya and Marjaneh, still in their robes, slipped off their scarves and their hair swayed in the balmy breeze. Marjaneh sat quietly, eyes closed and arms stretched wide to rest on the gunwales. She seemed to be enjoying the absolute freedom of the moment. Roya curled up next to her while Milan and Sepehr undressed to their swimsuits.

Roya and Milan talked to each other nonstop. This seemed to annoy Sepehr, who interrupted them every so often.

"I could stay here at this moment, forever," said Milan.

"Me too," said Roya.

"We should do this, you and I, live here for the rest of our lives," Milan continued.

"I wish I had my camera with me," said Sepehr. "I could take some great pictures."

"You could've taken a picture of us," Milan said.

Roya smiled. The more she saw him, the more comfortable she felt around him. She never blushed anymore. An image of his lean bare body was sculpted in her mind. Now, she could remember it for the rest of her life.

"I don't want to take a picture of you guys. I meant the setting sun, the moonlight," Sepehr said, agitated, his olive green eyes gleaming.

"Why wouldn't you take a picture of us?" Roya asked.

Marjaneh finally spoke. "Could you guys just shut up for a couple of minutes and let me enjoy this?"

The placid sea shifted colors, from blue to navy to black, as it swallowed the sun.

Sepehr turned to Milan, slung his arm around him, and squeezed his shoulder. "Ready to jump, my friend?"

"How about you two?" Milan asked the girls. Roya peeked over Milan's hands that gripped the wooden bench where he sat, their dark blue veins visible.

"We jump after you jump," Marjaneh responded.

Sepehr dove in, tired of waiting, as if he didn't care who went swimming. The boat rocked. Milan took a long leap after him and surfaced a few seconds later. "Coming in?" he yelled as he wiped his eyes and combed back his curly hair with his fingers.

Roya peered down at him. She grew up swimming alongside men, but since the revolution, when she was twelve, she hadn't been in a bathing suit in front of a man. She looked around, removed her robe, and kicked off her jeans and flip-flops. The evening breeze touched her bare skin and penetrated her turquoise swimsuit. For a moment she thought of the consequences. What if they were caught? What if Mamon and Baba found out? Especially after what had happened to her only a few months ago. The flogging. The pain. Yet for some strange, powerful reason, none of that mattered. At that moment she wanted to be wherever Milan was, in whatever condition, always and forever.

She dove.

Her scars jolted her as they were immersed into the sea. She stayed under the water for a second or two. When she lifted her head up, she turned to look at the boat and saw Marjaneh jumping.

The four of them swam, free from the world around them.

Marjaneh was a better skier than Roya, Sepehr a better photographer, and Milan a better pottery maker, but Roya was the best swimmer. She swam faster than the rest, her long strokes cutting through the water.

"Slow down," Milan shouted. "I want to swim with you."

Roya paused to let him catch up.

"It was my fault," he said, panting and reaching her. Now, it was just the two of them.

"What was your fault?"

"Did they leave scars?"

"It wasn't your fault."

"You were coming to see me."

"It wasn't your fault."

"Do you have scars?"

Roya halted and then floated on her back. "Yes," she said.

"Can I see them?"

Nobody but Mamon and Baba had seen her scars. She rolled on to her stomach and reached back to pull her hair away to expose them, but Milan's hand was already on her hair, tenderly drawing it aside. Roya closed her eyes and imagined the blue veins on his hands as he caressed her hair. It was the first time he was touching her.

"A boat!" screamed Sepehr. "A security boat, Pasdara."

Roya jerked. Her hair pulled away from Milan's hands. A searchlight on the horizon was pointed toward them. She panicked. She couldn't go through it again, to be able to tolerate it, the arrest, the humiliation, and the flogging. She couldn't put Mamon and Baba through it one more time. She and Milan swam as fast as they could back to the boat. She could hear him as he gasped for air and kept looking over her shoulder to make sure he was not falling too far behind. Finally they reached the boat, grabbed the rescue tube hanging over the side, and climbed aboard. Sepehr showed up a few seconds later, but there was no sign of Marjaneh.

"How far has she gone?" Roya said. "God … Marjaneh, Where are you?"

The sea was dark, the moonlight wasn't helping much, and they only had a single flashlight. Roya was scared, as scared as the time she spent in that gray room that reeked of urine, when she was arrested. The memory of the odor came to life, crawling up her nostrils. She never thought a smell could leave such a horrifying memory.

They started yelling, "Marjaneh, Marjaneh." A terrifying, endless minute later, she shouted back: "Here! I'm here!" Roya took a deep breath. The sea breeze cleared the stench from her mind.

"Stay right there. We're coming," Sepehr yelled.

The beaming light of the security boat was getting sharper. Sepehr started the engine while Milan and Roya dressed. They didn't bother drying off first. Dripping wet, her robe sucked to her skin. With her tongue, she licked the salty water off her lips. The boat drifted toward Marjaneh. Milan pulled her in, and Sepehr sped away. The security boat, now much closer, followed them. Marjaneh wanted to towel dry before putting on her clothes, but Sepehr protested. "Just put them on. Just put them on. They're getting close."

She had a hard time pulling up her pants. Water dripped off of her long hair as she put her head scarf on. Their little boat slashed through the dark. Lights along the beach lazily came to life as they neared.

"As soon as we get to the beach, you two must run as far

away as possible," Milan said. "They won't get to us before we get there. We're far enough." He gazed at Roya and continued, "I'm sorry."

She didn't ask for what. She knew.

"Promise me. Promise you'll take care of yourself," Milan went on.

"I promise," Roya said, not knowing when she would see him again.

Roya and Marjaneh dashed away from the boat. Marjaneh lost one of her flip-flops but continued to run. Roya's waterlogged clothes made it harder to move quickly.

"Shit. We left our towel," Marjaneh said as she took a deep breath.

"Just run," Roya said, gasping for air.

As they sprinted away from the beach, they decided to take a different route to avoid the White Plage, and eventually reached Freydon's Kabobi. It was already closed and all the lights were out, except for the red neon in the window that read: "Best Kabob by the Sea." Why was it closed? What time was it? Roya wondered, but she didn't want to pause or take a breath to ask Marjaneh, who, now, was a couple of steps behind. They probably were not in danger anymore, but they were late and Mamon and Baba would be worried.

Roya made a clumsy leap across an old metal bridge, which arched above a fast stream of water.

"Ouch!" Marjaneh screeched a couple of seconds later.

"What happened?" Roya said as she turned around.

Marjaneh was on the ground, her foot trapped in the metal bars. Pain contorted her face. "Ouch, ouch," she shrieked as Roya helped her to stand. Every time, Roya had crossed this damn bridge, she feared that her foot would jam in between its rusted iron rods.

"I'm OK. Let's go. I lost my other sandal too," she muttered and limped away. Roya grabbed her arm and placed it over her own shoulder. Marjaneh's jeans were ripped at the knee. She was bleeding.

Outside their villa, Mamon and Baba were waiting for them.

"What's going on? Where were you? Why are you soaking wet?" Baba asked, almost yelling.

She didn't know what to say. They hadn't planned this part.

"Oh my God, why are you bleeding?" Mamon asked Marjaneh. "Where are your sandals?"

"Not a big deal. I fell. We had dinner at Freydon's and then went for a walk. The water was so warm and nice that we decided to get a little wet, a quick swim with our clothes on," Marjaneh said as quickly as possible. She thought faster than Roya and was a better liar. "Then I fell crossing the rusty bridge and my flip-flops dropped in the water. Really, not a big deal. They were old anyways."

"Not a big deal?" Baba fumed. "Do you have any idea what time it is? You went swimming where you are not supposed to, where women can be arrested, and you say not a big deal. There are designated beaches for women and you know that. If something had happened to you, what was I going to tell your parents? You are my responsibility."

23

Roya had never seen Baba shout.

"We were worried to death. It's really late," Mamon said.

Baba shouted louder, pointing at Roya. "And you, don't stand there in silence. You were just in trouble. It wasn't your fault, but it is how it is now. How we have to live now. Didn't they just... Weren't you just ... You should know better. You are ..." He couldn't finish his sentence and then there was a bitter pause. Roya dropped her head and fidgeted with her fingers. Yes, of course she remembered, but she was going to see Milan again, no matter what. She would lie to Mamon and Baba again, if that was what it took to see him one more time. She would cheat the government rules. She wanted to see him. Again and again and again.

MIXED BLESSING

Michael Hardesty

Everything I was wearing was white: pants, belt, shirt, tie, socks and shoes. Even my underwear was white; a cotton tee and size 6c Jockey Juniors. Just my Mom and I knew that part. My Dad sure didn't. He was still sleeping as I dressed for my big day.

"Hurry on now," coaxed my mother in her kind and gentle voice: a voice that always made me want to comply. She was older than my schoolmates' moms, but that didn't matter to me. All my friends really liked her, and that made me proud.

"Is Dad coming?" I asked. "All the other kids' dads are going to be there."

"I'm not sure," she said, her tone still gentle, but now sweetly sad. "He wasn't feeling well at bedtime last night. I'll wake him in a few minutes and see how he's doing. I'm sure he'll want to go if he feels okay."

Most of the time Dad didn't feel okay. He was either drunk, sick with a hangover, or snoring in deep sleep. I heard Mom talking to him in their bedroom a few minutes later. Though I couldn't understand what they were saying, the tones of their voices made me know he wouldn't be coming with us. I moved closer to their door, wanting to hear what he was saying.

I heard my mother.

"It's not my idea, Harry. He asked me about it … mentioned the other kids' dads."

"I'm sick, goddammit, but if I weren't, I wouldn't want to watch him get indoctrinated with that Jesus stuff."

"Quiet! He'll hear you."

Mom and I walked the eight blocks to St. Columba, since we didn't have a car. About halfway there, the poorest family in our neighborhood, the Nortons, joined us for the walk. They didn't have a car either.

St. Columba Parish was the largest in the city's west end, and there were 115 first-grade, First Communicants. The church was originally built to be a gym, but I wouldn't have known that if Mom hadn't told me. 'St. C' was the only church I'd ever been in, and at the age of seven, I wasn't paying much attention to architecture or interior design. But indeed, its structure was merely a tiled rectangle, and I can certainly see now where the altar might have originally been conceived as a curtained stage behind one of the never-erected basketball goals.

So down the center aisle I walked that morning, with seven of the fourteen colorful Stations of the Cross on each side wall. I couldn't have been prouder had I been in St. Peter's Basilica or the Cathedral of Notre Dame. At the altar were a priest and an eighth-grade altar boy, both dwarfed by an enormous, lifelike replica of Jesus suffering on the cross.

As I knelt in front of the huge crucifix, I looked at Jesus and whispered, "I'm sorry my Dad's not here." Then, diverting my eyes from His, "You see, he's sick."

I'M FROM

Deborah Kevin

I'm from barbed-wired words,
that shredded my soul
leaving no external marks.
Invisible to others.

I'm from broken promises and
shattered dreams which
left me hiding on the bathroom floor
behind locked doors.

I'm from being pinned to the wall,
your eyes blazing,
spittle flying,
igniting my fight or flight.

I'm from unexpected visits,
shouting and shame.
Unfounded accusations
make me question my own sanity.

I'm from the stair landing, walls,
and ancient piano,
which stopped my forward momentum,
leaving me black and blue.

I'm from a car sitting hour after hour
outside my dark and shuttered home,
praying you'd just leave
without ever knocking.

I'm from the fear someone would notice
and the shame when they did,
not knowing what to say
to make them feel better.

I'm from questioning myself
and "How did this happen?"
Trying to understand
that which can't be.

I'm from confusing abuse
for love
because my childhood blueprint
was designed that way.

HUNTING THE DEVIL

- Chapter 1 -

Suanne Schafer

Dr. Jessica Hemings, Rwanda, April 10, 1994

Powered by a potent mixture of hatred and fear, Dr. Jessica Hemings darted from tree to tree, racing up one hill, down the next in the pitch-black night. She couldn't stop. Branches sliced her arms and legs. Stones bruised her feet. With every gasp, a side stitch lanced through her right ribs.

She glanced back. With that distraction, her feet tangled.

Down an embankment, Jess stumbled. Her feet fought for purchase on the slick water-soaked slope. Rocks rolled beneath her, making far too much noise. Sliding on her belly, she grabbed for a tree trunk to stop her free fall. After making so much racket, she held her breath and listened. No sounds of pursuit. She let her racing heart slow, caught her breath. Only then did she realize her right hand was empty. She'd lost the photograph of her children. She'd never find it in the dark. She closed her hand, now as empty as her heart. Her search would have to wait 'til first light.

She wasn't sure when she'd last heard the baying of the dogs tracking her. Maybe her pursuers had given up. For a moment, she could rest. She pulled herself semi-upright, then slumped against the tree, clutching her aching sides. She'd run the entire night. The thick brush around her provided good cover.

Two years ago, when she'd volunteered for a medical mission, Jess never dreamed that she'd be fleeing for her life among the *mille collines*, the thousand hills, of Rwanda. She had to get as far as possible from her clinic in Rwanteru Centre. The *Interahamwe*, the Rwandan paramilitary group, lay behind her. If she continued east, she'd reach the Kagera River and could cross to Tanzania—and safety.

As she sat, the eastern sky lightened. The rising sun made the fog look like watery milk. Jess caught the grumble of a straining motor. She peeked around the tree. A farm truck, packed with men rather than vegetables, chugged over the hill. Clothed in bright *dashikis* and beating their machetes in a steady rhythm

33

against the sides of the truck, the men inside could have been local farmers heading to work in their fields, but their raucous chants "Hutu *pawa*" and "Exterminate the *iyenzi*," revealed their identity and their mission. *Iyenzi* or "cockroaches" was the Hutu code word for Tutsis.

Damn! They were coming from the direction she was heading. That meant the militia stood both behind and ahead of her. She burrowed more deeply into the thicket and prayed for invisibility, remaining utterly still until their sounds faded.

Jess jerked awake, her arms and legs flailing. Her eyes snapped open. Shrieks still echoed in her ears. Who'd screamed? Wisps of dream-images faded. Then came the awareness that she'd uttered the cries.

After a moment's disorientation, she remembered where she was. And why. She looked up through tree branches. The sun was directly overhead. With everything that had happened in the past few days, she was surprised she'd slept.

Motionless, Jess remained hidden, listened, hoping no one had heard her screeches. She caught only the whisper of the wind, scattered bird calls, and the sporadic drip of water from the leaves. No human sounds. She slumped with relief and ran a hand through her hair. The humidity was so high her curls would have completely frizzed if they hadn't been so wet and dirty.

Her body ached—every bone, every muscle, every inch of skin—grim reminders of what she'd endured. Jess ventured a look downward. Thanks to Cyprien Gatera, she wore only a brown scrub top and a polka-dot bra, both ripped down the center front. He'd confiscated her pants and shoes, believing her nudity would prevent her escape. Along with her tawny skin, the dark scrub top had camouflaged her during the night, but after her tumble down the hillside, the shirt was so red with mud its true color was unrecognizable. She tried to lift the bra, but dried blood glued it to her chest. Insect bites covered her body. Black and blue marks shadowed her skin. Leaves stuck to her skin. Flies circled blackened scabs. She grimaced and flapped her hands in a vain effort to shoo them.

Next she looked at her feet. The muddy bottoms of her ladybug socks were shredded. Wincing, she peeled off the socks. Cuts and bruises covered her feet. Since she had no shoes, the ladybugs were the only protection her feet had, so she turned them heel side up and put them back on.

Jess turned her mind to her situation. For the first time since her escape, she had a few moments to plan her next move. Her wilderness skills were minimal. Hell, she hadn't even joined Philadelphia's Girl Scouts. She'd survive, damn it.

She just had to use her brain, her knowledge of basic human needs, not her fancy medical education.

Oxygen. No problem. She was breathing.

Water. For the moment the rain had stopped, but water dribbled from branches overhead and trailed down her forehead and nose. She licked her dry lips and opened her mouth to receive the drops. In April, the height of the long rainy season, water was readily available. Its potability was her main concern. Groundwater in Rwanda teemed with microorganisms guaranteed to give her dysentery. She gulped. Even diarrhea was preferable to the fate she'd escaped.

Food. Humans could live longer without food than water, but her last meal had been over twenty-four hours ago—her stomach grumbled in agreement—and being on the run burned calories at a rapid clip. Petite and maxing out at 110 pounds, she didn't have much reserve. Tomorrow at the latest she had to eat.

Shelter. That was less a concern than avoiding detection. Though located just south of the equator, Rwanda's high altitude resulted in autumn temperatures ranging from the sixties at night to eighties during the day. In her soaked top, she was uncomfortably cool but not cold enough to worry about hypothermia, especially once she got moving.

With a grimace, Jess fought down memories of Gatera and what he'd had done to her two adopted children, to her clinic staff, her patients, to her. She swayed at the thought of the blood. Blood on the wall. Blood on the floor. Blood on her. She drew those thoughts into a tight ball of black-hot hate. No matter how long it took, she'd get the bastard. Even if she had to kill him herself. In uncharacteristic visions, which were disturbingly satisfying, she hacked him to bits with a machete.

Jess had been aware of growing unrest in Rwanda, but the US Embassy and PARFA, the relief agency she worked for, had assured her she wouldn't be affected. When Hutu extremists began killing their political opponents, Americans weren't being targeted. By the time the American Embassy called saying to evacuate, it was too late. Gatera had already commandeered her clinic.

Now, Jess's goal was to reach Rusumo Falls and cross the border. She crawled from her hiding place. Her aching body made every motion an effort. When she stood, a wave of pain made her wish she'd moved more slowly. With her first step, she winced. Her upside-down socks were no help.

Once again conscious that she wore only a ripped hospital scrub top, Jess tugged its ragged edges together. Naked otherwise, she was vulnerable to the *Interhamwe* rampaging through the land. For that matter, to any male who happened by. Mentally she added shoes and clothes, along with food and some sort of weapon, to her list of supplies to steal.

Before she did anything, she had to find the photo of her kids. It was all she had left of them. She searched the trajectory of her fall, and when sunlight glanced off the white paper, she found it, limp and soggy from exposure to the overnight rain. Jess picked up the fragile photograph, trying to brand her babies' faces into her memory before the image disintegrated. The anguish Jess had been suppressing exploded through her. An animal-like wail, the sound of her sorrow, resounded through the forest.

Something crashed through nearby trees. Fearing Gatera had found her, Jess raced to her prior hiding place. Jess's breathing became so rapid she felt dizzy. Her heart galloped in her chest. Her fingers tingled. As a physician, she recognized the signs of an anxiety attack. She needed to rein in her terror and grief to remain calm. If she panicked, she'd certainly fall into Gatera's hands.

Inhale. Hold. Exhale.

Every time she thought she had herself under control,

memories of her children surfaced. Over and over she fought those thoughts down and started her breathing exercises anew. Inhale. Hold. Exhale.

Whatever had made the noise never appeared. She was over-reacting to the earlier stimulus. Slowly, her hysteria subsided. Word choice?

To survive Rwanda's current chaos, Jess would have to concentrate on her surroundings. The sounds of birds chirping, animals scuttling in the brush, the scent of the wet earth and fallen leaves, even the whispering of the trees themselves, filled her senses. Defiantly, she straightened her shoulders. She'd survive—somehow—to beat her enemy at his own game and bring him to justice.

Gatera would expect Jess to head due east. Limping, she headed north, avoiding roads, remaining in the forest as much as possible. Lake Cyambwe was fifteen miles north as the crow flies from Rwanteru Centre. If she hit the settlements around the lake, she'd know she'd gone too far. As she crested one *colline,* a cloud of smoke stained the sky an oily black above the next hill. Another burnt village. If the *Interhamwe* had already passed through, she should be safe and could scavenge for the provisions she needed.

Her calves aching from climbing, Jess headed toward the village. A shriek disturbed the sounds of the forest. It sounded like a baby's cry. But that couldn't be. A wild animal? Nothing lethal, though. Lions and other predators were limited to the western game preserves. She crouched behind several boulders. The sound grew nearer. Cautiously she peeked from the rocks.

Women, dressed in colorful fabrics, walked rapidly by, carrying babies on their backs, balancing toddlers on one hip, and dragging youngsters by the hand. A mother popped her nipple into the wailing child's mouth to hush it. Others balanced baskets of food on their heads or pushed handcarts loaded with household goods, produce, and chickens. One little girl, wearing one pink sandal, limped on her bare foot. Older children tugged goats or carried jerry cans of water or bunches of bananas as big as themselves. This wasn't the usual band of women carrying hoes and rakes and chatting merrily as they headed to work the fields. These were refugees, loaded with their worldly goods, fleeing the *Interahamwe*. But they were heading west, away from the border. Where had they come from? And more importantly, where did they think they could go to escape the militia?

After they passed, Jess resumed her trek, following the smoke. As she approached, she dodged behind trees and bushes to remain out of sight. The humidity pressed the sweet odor of cooking meat close to the ground. Her mouth watered. Her stomach grumbled.

On the outskirts, she paused, looking and listening. Laundry, fluttering from tree branches, gave a sense of normalcy offset by an unnatural silence. Not a single human voice. Not even the twittering of birds. Just the crackling of flames from burning huts. Oddly, not every house was aflame. The *Interahamwe* had only burned Tutsi homes. Someone had collaborated with the militia and singled out Tutsis.

Cautiously, Jess slipped through the narrow space between two rough mud-brick houses and peeked into the main street.

She wasn't sure what she'd expected—certainly not what lay before her. Bodies—men, women, children, babies—were strewn haphazardly about, left where they'd been cut down by machetes. Jess started to dash to their aid. She stopped herself. She couldn't do any good if she were captured. Fists clenched, she forced herself to remain in place.

Minutes passed.

Something crept from behind a house.

A dog.

Jess's shoulders slumped in relief.

She waited. Nothing else moved.

The canine approached a body, sniffed, then buried his teeth in the corpse's open wound.

Unable to contain her horror, Jess shuddered at the ripping sound of flesh being torn from another human. She grabbed a large rock. Her first toss missed. Blindly she reached for another. When it felt too light to be a stone, she glanced at what she held in her hand. A small pink sandal. She prayed the toddler she'd seen an hour earlier hadn't seen this horror. She cast the shoe aside and hurled a second stone. Again she missed—barely.

The dog raised his head, turned toward her, and snarled.

Her third stone struck the animal on the flank.

With a yelp and a menacing growl, he slunk into the forest.

Jess waited for several minutes before entering the village. Immediately she searched for survivors, checking all the bodies. With each, she closed eyes frozen in horrified gazes. The *Interahamwe* had cut the tendons in their victims' legs so they couldn't run, then amputated each extremity, inflicting the most possible pain. Blood stained the rust-colored earth a darker red. The women, their clothing flung above their waists, had been raped and their breasts cut off before being killed.

She couldn't understand the slaughter. The militia killed people simply because they were Tutsi or moderate Hutu who opposed the Hutu extremists. Among her patients, as many Hutu looked Tutsi as Tutsi looked Hutu. Tutsis were just as poor as Hutus. Their houses were identical. The terraced fields they farmed identical. The lack of health care and education identical. Jess had never been able to tell the two groups apart. The locals couldn't either. Ethnicity was based on identity cards the Belgians issued in 1933 that classified every individual as Tutsi, Hutu, or Twa. Sixty years later, those same ID cards allowed *génocidaires* to readily identify their prey.

As Jess knelt beside yet another body, a moan almost too low to hear, snagged her attention. Quickly, she glanced around. Where had the sound come from? She palpated the spread-eagled woman's carotid artery. No pulse. Next to the corpse, a boy lay face-down. Jess searched for his heartbeat. It was weak and thready. She tenderly turned him over.

Snakes writhed beneath his body.

Jess recoiled.

Then shook her head. Not snakes. Worse. Far worse. Intestines spilling from a deep slash in his abdomen. The boy's genitals had been amputated. He'd dragged himself to his mother's side, embedding dirt into his wounds and leaving a trail of blood.

He groaned, the sound extraordinarily loud in the quiet.

Her guts clenched. He was only eight or nine years old.

Who could possibly do such vile things to a child? No one she'd categorize as human. She understood the politics, the history between Hutu and Tutsi, but couldn't understand how it led to mutilating fellow human beings. Leaders who conceived of such atrocities should be shot.

Jess looked at her hands. They were filthy. She glanced around. No way to wash them. What she wouldn't give for some hand sanitizer right now. But it didn't matter. She had no treatment to offer the boy, no surgical instruments, no antibiotics. It wasn't fair. Despite eight years of medical training, she couldn't save him. He was doomed to a slow painful death.

Jess ran her hands over the boy's head. His whimpers lessened at her touch. The Hippocratic Oath flashed though her mind. *Do no harm.* This child had mere hours to live. If she stayed to care for him, she risked recapture. He was too big for her to carry. Transporting him to safety would inflict more pain without improving his prognosis. Yet she couldn't abandon him. She shook her head. She hated to admit it. Only one option remained.

Wiping tear streaks from the boy's face, she pulled his head into her lap. "I promise you'll join your family soon." Visions of her year-old twins flashed before her. They'd had the same smooth cheeks and rich dark skin as this boy. No! If she thought of them right now, she'd go insane. She shoved those memories into the deepest vault of her mind and slammed the door.

Jess closed her eyes, placed her hand over the boy's mouth and nose, and pressed firmly into his round face.

"Go-away-go-away-go-away!"

The raucous cry jerked Jess back to the moment. She'd lived in Rwanda long enough to recognize the call of a go-away bird. She opened her eyes. Looked down. Her hand still covered the boy's face. Without releasing pressure, she felt for his pulse. Nothing. She slumped in relief. The child was dead. A lifetime had passed—literally—in the moments she'd been there. She lifted her hand and stared at her shaking fingers. Trained to save lives, she'd just—

"*Go away-go-away-go-away!*" The bird repeated its call.

No time for Jess to mourn the life she'd had just taken. She needed to take the bird's advice and get moving. She locked memories of this boy—and what she'd done to him—into the vault with her children.

Jess rose, unsteady on her feet, and studied the village. Heat waves danced in the humid air as flames enveloped the thatched roofs of several huts. She gagged with the realization that the cooking odor was the charred flesh of people trapped inside burning homes. She slammed her eyes tight, shutting out the sight, then forced herself to lift her lids. No time to wallow in emotions. She must focus on survival.

The intact structures must have belonged to Hutus, but even they had abandoned their village. Anyone who wasn't dead had evacuated, taking all they could carry. She'd be lucky to find a single item on her list.

Jess peered through the open door of a nearby hut. Bodies sprawled across the floor. The dead couldn't harm her, so she entered, tiptoeing around the corpses. The pools of blood made life unlikely, but she checked to be sure they were truly dead. She was a rational woman, didn't believe in ghosts, yet as she scavenged for supplies, she swore ghostly hands clawed at her ankles, stroked her arms, fluttered through her hair, kissed her face. A chill ran from her neck to the bottom of her spine. Digging through the jettisoned belongings of strangers was creepy. She found a tattered t-shirt several sizes too big. In the next hut, a dented pot, a wooden spoon, and a large knife.

Everywhere she found food, she stole it—sweet potatoes, bananas, plantains. Nearly every home had cassava roots, but she had no idea how to prepare them to get rid of the natural cyanide. She devoured a pot of *ugali* on the spot, even the burnt parts, though the cold glutinous cornmeal mush stuck in her dry throat.

From the laundry she'd seen as she entered the village, she chose several rectangular strips of cloth, *kangas*, that could serve as anything from a shawl to a skirt to a backpack.

Somehow the dead watched Jess's every move, their eyes following her as she raided their few belongings. For a semblance of privacy, she hid between two buildings before removing her ripped scrub top and socks. One length of fabric she fashioned into a skirt. She tossed her scrub top, bra, and ladybug socks into a flaming hut, watching until they incinerated. If the *Interahamwe* found them, they'd know a foreigner had been there.

Suddenly Jess had an idea. Maybe she could deceive the dogs by wearing shoes marked with other people's scents. She returned to the corpses and removed sandals from anyone who remotely wore her size. Her planned deception didn't keep her from shuddering as she wiggled her feet into the sandals she'd stripped from a dead woman.

After a last look around, she bound her possessions in another cloth and returned to the forest.

SIGNS

John Maly

The leaves dropping off of our red maple tree,
The browning edge of the lily flower,
Your nearly empty glass of chablis,
Keep us ever-mindful of the hour.

As the sun drops down through the west windowpane
And the last water drains from our bath,
Darkness builds despite prayers made in vain,
Slowing for neither pleas nor for wrath.

The look you saw in your doctor's eyes,
The nurse's voice in practiced sympathy,
Signs of what you by now must surmise,
Fulfillment of nature's cruelest guarantee.

Our lifetime of planning, the fates now impugn,
We face dreams you'll no longer partake in.
Yet still we speak of seeing Paris next June,
In spite of what our hearts just won't take in.

And then, it's soon now, and you will not eat.
They're upping your dosage times two.
You sleep then repeat, your face weary, as sweet.
I've never before not known what to do

IF NOT WORDS

Roy Dufrain

I think of 1978 as my Kerouac period. Before that was my blustery Hemingway period, and afterward my disastrous Hunter S. Thompson period. But '78 was Kerouac, and in the spring I drifted out of college and began to dream of going on the road.

Of course, I needed a Neal Cassady—a running buddy like the mad ones that Kerouac famously shambled after and wrote about—"the ones who are mad to live, mad to talk, mad to be saved, desirous of everything at the same time, the ones who never yawn or say a commonplace thing, but burn, burn, burn like fabulous yellow roman candles exploding like spiders across the stars."

That was what I needed. What I had was Pat Kelly.

I first met Pat in Lupoyoma City, a small poor town next to a big green lake three hours north of San Francisco. He was the new kid in eighth grade, from Texas by way of San Jose, with a junkie father locked up in San Quentin and his fortyfiveish mother shuttling drinks at the Weeping Willow Resort & Trailer Court. I won't go into it here but, at the time, I was in a murky state of social exile myself due to a local scandal involving my family. What drew me to Pat was our shared status as temporary outsiders, and the fact that he was completely unimpressed by Lupoyoma gossip. That just wasn't how he measured the world.

I met him because our American History teacher sentenced him to three swats for "cracking wise." The teacher had a thick wooden paddle drilled with holes to reduce wind resistance. Pat rose from his backrow desk and said, "Now, how much history do you think I can learn from three swats?" He was taller and older than the rest of us. Straight blondish hair, parted down the middle and tucked behind jughandle ears. Tank top shirt and wide bellbottoms over black motorcycle boots, and his wallet on a silvery chain secured to a belt loop. He took long gangly strides to the front of the classroom, with his chin up and his shoulders back.

The teacher glowered. "Make it five then."

Pat faced the class and grabbed his ankles. The teacher swung for the fences. Pat overacted a mockish "Ow!" with every blow, and the teacher tacked on another two swats—to zero effect on

Pat's demeanor. I had a front row desk, and after the final swing Pat straightened up and flashed his wide floppy grin right at me, then earnestly advised the teacher to watch the Jack LaLanne show. I laughed. Then the whole class laughed. The teacher pointed at the door and ordered both of us to the principal's office. On the way out Pat paused at the threshold, looked back across the room and said, "Seven a.m., Channel 3," with a big wink, and turned out the door. He had something I hadn't seen before—an attitude or quality I admired, even coveted, but couldn't name at first.

In those days I collected baseball cards and words—words I read or heard and wanted to remember or accrue to my character. I had the young idea that words had a way of adding up to a man, and I wanted to choose the right ones. Words that said, listen, and rang the air like silver struck crystal. I wrote down their definitions in a reporter's notebook that was spiral-bound and narrow, with pages that flipped rather than turned. My father was the editor of the town newspaper, and I'd stolen the notebook from his dour, disciplined office. I kept it under my bed in a Keds shoebox with the baseball cards.

Exultation was the word I collected for Pat. Triumphant joy. He measured his world in degrees of exultation though he'd likely never seen the word. It was a way of being in the world that I wanted to understand and claim for myself. Late on a school night, with the rest of the house quiet and dark, I sat cross-legged on my bed with the paperback dictionary splayed open in a circle of lamplight and copied the definition into the reporter's notebook.

We ran together all that school year, in creeks and alleys and neglected vacant lots, in parks and ball fields and quarter arcades. Cut classes to fish by the sunny lake, trespassed in empty, dilapidated houses and burglarized the Little League snack shack. Partners in boyish crime.

Once, we kind of stole a car. Just a daytime joyride around the pockmarked backstreets of Lupoyoma in a big Chevy station wagon that belonged to some girl's mom. That girl would do anything for Pat. If she didn't, another girl would. But the mom did not feel the same, and neither did the city police. Their entire fleet of vehicles—all three—converged on the station wagon at a four-way intersection. Black-and-white Fords and spinning red lights to our left, right, and rear. The street in front of us was clear—Pat could've gunned it and started a chase, but he calmly pulled over, put the car in park and turned off the engine.

"Oh shit, we're going to jail, my dad's gonna kill me," I said.

Pat grinned and shrugged, "Win some, lose some, partner."

Between us on the green vinyl bench seat, the girl was sobbing. Pat put his arm around her, gently tilted her head and kissed the top of it. "Don't worry, darlin'," he said, in that Texifornia drawl. Then he opened the car door and stepped out like a fifteen-year-old man.

The girl and I were immediately cast by the presiding adults as good kids under a bad influence, and we were ordered out of the way as officers handcuffed Pat and marched him toward one of the police cars—chin up and shoulders back.

I heard around town that he was sent to the notorious Bottlerock Ranch, the closest thing to reform school in

Lupoyoma County. I didn't see him until a year later, the day we became cousins. Well, my cousin married his cousin, and Pat figured that made me and him cousins too. I still don't know if that's correct, but such technicalities were not Pat's concern. From that day on, whenever I ran into him, whenever he spotted me in a crowd—at family weddings or funerals, July picnics, or drunken teen parties—he'd always wave his arms and holler out, "Cousin! How the hell are ya!" He never lost that thing I was trying to pin words on, even with the cops always on his case and rarely more than ten bucks and a wink to his name.

I graduated from Lupoyoma High in '75, but Pat already had his G.E.D. and loved to remind me that he earned it at continuation high solely by reading through their collection of Louis L'amour. When I told him I was going away to college, he pshawed and said, "Cousin, you're doin' it the hard way."

Emmalita Romero was somehow immune to Pat Kelly's charms. In 1978, she and I were scholarship kids, chasing upward mobility at the small, ivy-aspiring University of the Pacific in Stockton. We had met in Economics 101, which Emmalita eventually aced and I did not complete. We lived off-campus in a rickety one-bedroom apartment on a dead-end street—and in sin, as her father regularly assured us. One February twilight Pat showed up like a long-lost one-man surprise party. Screeched and skidded to the curb in a dusty copper Lincoln borrowed from his mom's latest boyfriend. Early sixties Continental, low to the ground and half a block long, with suicide doors. He honked "shave and a haircut—two bits," leapt out of the car, raced around to the passenger side and made a great show of mock chivalry holding the door for a bleach-blonde teenager who emerged waving a fifth of gold tequila above her head. Emmalita and I stood on the brick front steps, both shaking our heads, only one of us smiling. Pat turned to me, opened his arms wide and cried out, "Cousin! How the hell are ya!"

Emmalita muttered something in Spanish and rolled her eyes in my direction.

I gave her a palms-up shrug.

We all got tremendously drunk shooting tequila at the second-hand kitchen table with the blue paint peeling off and the raw wood starting to show. Pat and I took turns telling tales of our juvenile exploits as if they were Homeric epics. Needling each other and arguing over details until we ended up out front on the community lawn in a clumsy, laughable wrestling match.

"Boys," Emmalita said, categorically.

The blonde turned out to be Pi-Delta-something. Pat had sugar-talked her right off the steps of the sorority house, and at some point, he slipped her out the back door and was balling her from behind, right on the little porch, bent over the wooden railing with a panoramic view of the parking lot—the February cold be damned.

It was Emmalita who opened the door and discovered them. She yanked it shut in a hurry. "What the hell!" she said. "He's fucking her on the back porch!"

I tried to smile. "We did it there once, remember?" I slid my arms around her waist.

"It's our porch!" she said, slamming me in the chest with both hands.

Emmalita stomped off to bed, the Pi-Delta blonde passed out on the couch, and Pat and I stayed up and finished off the tequila. The blurry dawn caught us still at the kitchen table, commiserating and confessing. Or was that just me? I vaguely remember reading out loud from *On the Road* and resolutely proclaiming, "I'm sick of teachers you have to call Doctor. They act like they can write a prescription for your whole fucking future. Here, kid, take two Aristotles and call me in the morning."

"Ya worry too much," Pat said. "Always did. Come look me up in Santa Barb this summer. Gonna get me a landscaping job, probably get you one too. Gonna build rock walls for rich ladies whose husbands ain't home." He shot me a big wink and laughed.

"Yeah, right," I said. But the possibility took up residence in my mind and hibernated there the rest of the winter.

When spring came around, I received a postcard advertising a bar and restaurant called The Palms, in the town of Carpinteria, just down the coast from Santa Barbara. On the front there was a blue-sky picture of a whitewashed building rimmed with green cornices and fronted by a row of towering palm trees. "The Palms" was painted in voluptuous green script arcing high across the white bricks. On the back, the address of the place, the canceled stamp, and in Pat's half-schooled printing, "The weather is here, wish you were beautiful! Ha!"

I didn't show the postcard to Emmalita. I tucked it between the pages of my broken spine paperback of *On The Road* and shelved the book in our "library" made of salvaged boards and stolen milk crates. According to legend, Neal Cassady sent an eighteen-page, sixteen-thousand-word letter to Kerouac that transformed his writing forever. What I got was a nine-word postcard with no return address.

Still, I considered it an invitation—and a map of sorts.

It was late April and late Thursday night, and I had everything except my toothbrush in the new backpack. Two changes of clothes, three harmonicas, two Kerouacs, one Kesey, my old paperback dictionary, two hundred bucks rolled up in a sock, the postcard from Pat, and my reporter's notebook with room for a few more words. I promised myself they would be words of change and becoming, not the cautious preparation of academia. I leaned the backpack against the wall next to the front door—bright orange nylon, shiny aluminum frame, army surplus mummy bag lashed on, and I told Emmalita, "I want to be on that on-ramp with my thumb out no later than seven in the morning to catch those business guys headed for San Francisco."

She'd been in the bathroom almost an hour showering and getting ready for bed. She came into the living room wearing the white full slip that always knocked me out. Nothing underneath. Long black hair dripping wet. "Baby, it's a twenty minute walk to the freeway," she said, "even more with that heavy thing on your back. You can sleep in, and I'll drive you in the vee-dub before I go to class." She slinked across the carpet, and her smile was dressed in red lipstick. She pushed me back on the sofa, pulled off my t-shirt and shorts and straddled me in the white slip. She shushed me when I opened my mouth to speak—and that was probably a good thing because I might have said I love you.

Emmalita didn't indulge in that kind of talk. Traditional monogamous relationships were obsolete. She was a liberated Chicana who read Betty Friedan and Simone de Beauvoir, and had marched with César Chávez. She dismissed Kerouac as one of the last great chauvinist pigs, but she listened when I read aloud on long car rides and in our bed on hot Stockton nights unfit for sleep or love. "You get so excited over these words," she would say, like a new mother saying, "Aw, so cute." But I would ignore that and talk about the blue echoes of Coltrane's saxophone in the syncopated rhythms of Kerouac's prose, and the way it spoke to me that he rejected button-down society to search for his own meaning across the map of America.

When I'd called my father to say that I was dropping out of school to go on the road, he'd offered me a job at the newspaper. But when I told Emmalita, she understood. (I kept Pat Kelly's name out of it.) We were sitting on the red brick stairs by the front door in the early evening, the bricks still warm from the afternoon heat. We brought out bottles of beer and watched the sun slide into the low skyline across the valley. I showed her the new summer catalog from the university, with the fake snapshots of students at internships, posing with stethoscopes, clipboards and briefcases like children playing dress-up. I pointed and jabbed at the pictures and said, "That's not me. That's not me. That's not me either. I'm not in there."

Emmalita nodded and took a long sip of beer. She didn't try to talk me out of it or lecture me like a parent. "Go," she said, still looking out across the rooftops. "I could never forgive myself if you don't. And after graduation I'll be leaving to law school who knows where." She picked at the bottle's label with a fingernail. "We're young. We each have our own dreams."

We didn't want to live our parents' lives, tangled forever in regret and resentment. We agreed they were childish, and it was a satisfying irony that we were so adult in our acceptance of individual freedom. She even promised to store my records and books—including my stack of rare blues albums and the first edition Hemingway I'd found at a yard sale.

The day I left, I woke up in near darkness, alone in bed, with the feeling that I was already late. I found Emmalita at the kitchen stove frying chorizo and eggs, still in the white slip. She looked at me sweetly over her shoulder. "Your favorite," she said.

"We don't have time for breakfast," I said, but she just turned back to the pan and stirred with the flat wooden spoon. The smell of chorizo rose in the steam.

"You know he never found it," she said. "He drank himself to death. All that going and going and he never found the meaning of anything."

I sat down at the kitchen table and studied her. So beautiful and smart and sure-hearted, so luminous of purpose. That was the word I'd written in the notebook, watching her the first day of Econ 101, already pestering the professor with feminist critiques. Luminous. Shedding light. Now I memorized the hair rolling down her back in black waves, her shoulders warmed to gold by the light of the one bare bulb in the ceiling, her shape moving under the slip like a liquid silhouette, the reflection of the light bulb trembling in her eyes.

I still had to go.

It was eight-forty by the time we got to the freeway, and a rare spring fog had crawled in off the delta. The commuters were long gone, and two bums had already taken positions up the on-ramp. Emmalita pulled over and left the engine running. She gripped the steering wheel and stared straight ahead while I maneuvered my pack out of the back seat. I walked around to her window. She rolled it down and turned her face to me. Her eyes were wet. I looked down at the ground and said, "Thanks for the ride."

She said, "Will you even miss me?"

"Of course," I said, and bent down to kiss her.

She reached out the window and slapped me so hard I saw floating spots.

"*Estúpido cabrón!*" she said. "You will miss me. You will come back, and I won't be here. And if you don't come back I will scratch all your records and burn your *Old Man and The Sea*. Pendejo!"

Her rear tires spit gravel as she sped away.

I trudged up the on-ramp past the two bums so as not to steal first position, which I knew would violate hitchhiker etiquette. At the time I knew that and little else about citizenship of the road. My older stepsister had started me young with daytrips thumbing around Lupoyoma County, but I had never ventured an overnight trip before. Now I would trace one small piece of Kerouac's map—if I could make it out of Stockton.

58

The fog was tentacled, the cold insidious. The bum in second position hunkered down on a bedroll in a tattered fatigue jacket. I stood and blew into my cupped hands. The first-position bum watched with gristled detachment. I use the word "bum" because "homeless" wasn't established as the preferred euphemism in 1978. Drifter sounds too nefarious, hobo too clichéd, wanderer too soft-focus. And these appeared to be respectable bums—not recreational or philosophically ambitious, not the dharma bums or wino savants of Kerouac, but respectable nonetheless. When I walked past, each of them offered a chin nod to acknowledge my good manners.

A car or sometimes two at a time came up the on-ramp every few minutes. It was not a steady stream. I stood shivering with my head bowed, shifting pebbles with the toe of my boot. Then a car would appear, and the two bums and I would present ourselves, one-two-three, in rapid sequence. The bum in the first position wore a blue knit cap and was stooped and gray-stubbled. He held up his right hand as if measuring an inch between his thumb and forefinger to show that he only needed to go a mile or two. The bum on the bedroll was younger. He stood up and let his arm hang down with his hand below his hip, his thumb angled out with cool indifference. Then me, standing lock-kneed with my arm perpendicular to the road and my eager thumb almost quivering. I made eye contact with every driver, recalling my high school counselor's interview advice.

A truck stopped and picked up the gray-stubbled bum. He nodded through the window as he rode past. The other bum picked up his bedroll and walked down to the old bum's spot. He sat down, then looked up and waved me toward him. When I got there he said, "Where ya headed?"

"Santa Barb," I said, trying to sound suitably traveled, "actually Carpinteria."

"Headed down the coast myself," he said, and took some time to look me over. I became hotly aware of my new orange pack, my brightly washed overalls and clean farm bureau work boots, my peach fuzz face and the girlish dark hair flowing down to my shoulders. Bangles. Yes, I wore bangles.

The bum said, "Wanna go together?"

I must have looked confused.

"Sometimes it's better with two guys."

"Oh."

"People think it's easier to be crazy alone."

"Yeah."

He put out his hand. "Name's Terry."

He wore a red bandana headband over unruly curls of rusty brown hair, and his unfinished beard reminded me of my grandmother's windowsill cactus. He had dark squinting eyes and a handshake that read like a swim at your own risk sign. He said he'd been on the road for years. He'd never been outside North Carolina before the army, but he'd come back from Vietnam with a spiteful heroin habit to kick and a desire to see the country. "See what I was killing for," he said.

Here was a piece of the America I thought I was looking for, the sad and true but unbroken America you couldn't find in a dorm room or a library stall. Or in a rickety apartment playing house with a future lawyer. Or the dusty office of a Podunk newspaper. I now felt that I was officially on the road although I hadn't managed a single ride. I could see myself on a barstool at The Palms, regaling Pat Kelly with exaggerated tales of my tremendous adventures with Terry the All-American bum.

The sun burned through the fog, then started in on us. Terry had a pair of aviator sunglasses that might've been stolen off Douglas MacArthur himself. Dark green lenses and gold wire frames with the looping ear stem. We finally got a ride from a freckled high school kid in a 65 Ford Econoline van. Terry sat shotgun with one elbow out the window, with his windblown hair and red bandana, and the reflections of the highway speeding across those sunglasses. I climbed in the back and sat on a lumpy mattress covered with a ratty brown bedspread. We rumbled west across the great San Joaquin Valley, straight at the sun.

I dipped into the money sock, handed the kid a ten, and Terry convinced him to let us sleep in the van, parked on the street outside his parents' house in a monochromatic subdivision. But the parents got wise, and we were rousted out around dawn, the panicky dad pounding on the side doors until we emerged, then threatening us down the street with a golf club. Nine-iron, I think.

We crossed the southern arm of the gray-spackled San Francisco Bay that afternoon on a long, low bridge like a highway upon the water. Terry had a Vietnam buddy who owned a bar in San Carlos. It was a surly looking place surrounded by chopped and raked Harley Davidsons. Terry marched through the swinging door like no big deal, and I fell in warily behind him. Every head in the bar swiveled to stare us down. Terry's buddy was a stone outcrop of a man called Sergeant Oliver. Dark straight hair down to his belt, wild thick beard and a big bearish laugh. "You better stick to yourselves," he said. "My regulars don't take to outsiders, and I got no time to save your ass. Again." He laughed and confined us to the storeroom with a deck of cards and a bottle of house bourbon. But, by his own admission, Terry was not a reliable follower of orders. And I was following him. We slipped out when Sergeant Oliver was busy, and Terry made fast friends of the whole crowd by sharing the bourbon and losing at pool. I played harmonica along with Free Bird on the jukebox, and after we helped close up the place, Sergeant Oliver locked us in, and we slept like ragged children curled up in the red leather tuck-n-roll booths.

The next day we got sidetracked and stranded in the farming town of Watsonville, where it rained like hell was water. Terry somehow knew where to hop the fence at the city yard, and we clambered over and sought shelter in huge sections of concrete culvert. There were dozens of these cylinders big as railroad boxcars, laid out in tidy rows waiting for some major construction project. I followed Terry, and we ducked into one. Inside it was all cozy echoes, outside nothing but the hiss and patter of rain… until we heard the low snarl of the watchdog. Then it was a cartoon-scramble back over the fence and a half-mile jog to an all-night laundromat where we shivered all night soaked through and nodding in yellow plastic chairs shaped like your butt.

I relished every minute of these complications and travails, and harbored the furtive belief that some holy chemistry of fate was involved in appointing Terry the All-American bum as the patron saint of my road.

In Big Sur, now four days gone from Stockton, we chanced on a woodsy encampment beside the highway, where nearly thirty fellow travelers were set up. This confluence of meandering souls seemed to call for a suitable commemoration. A tiny shack of a store stood across the highway, someone's weather-beat hat was passed around camp like a collection plate, and the fire, whiskey and talk burned late into the night. I pulled out a harp and jammed blues with a sunburnt old picker from Show Low, Arizona. Terry met a frizzy haired hippie woman headed up to Mendocino to make pottery, and I believe he spent some time in her sleeping bag. I scribbled the definition of confluence in my notebook. Where two or more streams or paths become one.

I don't remember lying down to sleep. I do remember waking up, alone, the contents of my pack dumped on the ground, the money sock stretched out, empty. There's enough regret and disillusion already built into a hangover without robbery in the bargain. I never saw Terry again. But I found the aviator sunglasses in a pocket of my backpack—a weak apology I concluded, and tucked them away in the pouch of my overalls. Blood-eyed and down to seventeen dollars, I nursed my pride in the woods of Big Sur all day, then slept troubled under a three-quarter moon.

There was a phone booth next to the little store, and in the morning I sat cross-legged on the nearby lawn and eavesdropped on a few weary and desperate phone calls. Maybe Emmalita would wire me some money back in Monterey. It would mean surrender, but I could catch a Greyhound and drowse in her arms that very evening. I rehearsed the entire call in my head, playing both parts, her finger-wagging satisfaction and my red-faced shame.

I thought of the postcard from Pat Kelly with the sunlight flashing off the bricks of The Palms. I'd told Terry I had family in Carpinteria who were expecting me. But Pat was not expecting me. I hadn't seen him but once in the past year. I had nothing to go on but that sunny photo and my own restlessness.

I thought of my father.

"A pipe dream," he had said. He'd offered me advice as well as a job. "Son, you won't learn how to write on the side of the goddamn road."

"I might learn what to write," I said.

But my father was an editor, not a writer. Words were either essential or expendable, and always in relation to a specific and utilitarian purpose—science, commerce, the news. In his mind, fiction was a toy made of words.

He'd scoffed and shook his head. "Might as well stick that thumb up your ass."

But now I got up off the ground and pulled out the MacArthur sunglasses and put them on like a coat of armor. I strapped on the dusty orange backpack, walked over to the southbound lane and stuck my thumb out for the next car. My hand low against my hip.

Two days further down the coast, I had a ride that would have taken me all the way to Carpinteria, but I got out five miles short in the tiny town of Summerland—because Kerouac had once spent the night on the beach there. I hunted up a liquor store and spent my last folding money on a half-pint of Southern Comfort and a family-size can of pork and beans.

I walked to the beach in the Summerland twilight. I made a driftwood fire, ate the beans out of the can with my pocketknife and sipped the sweet liquor like sacrament. There is a certain bliss contained in the moment when one owns a full belly and a full bottle at the same time, even if one also owns an empty wallet. I was bleary and beat and alone without a dollar to dream on, and yet I had the tremendous sense that all was right. In that hour, on that beach, on the map of my heart, I crossed paths with Kerouac.

I thought of that word, tremendous, because it appears so often in *On the Road*, and in so many contexts that you begin to think he was spraying it around as decoration, unconscious of its specific meaning. I got out the paperback dictionary and read the definition by the firelight: "very great in amount, scale, or intensity." The root was the Latin word for tremble, and it made me think that Kerouac knew exactly what he was doing, consciously or not. He wanted to suffuse his prose with that deep underlying sensitivity. To bequeath his own shudder at the amount, scale and intensity of America, the world and life. He wanted us to ingest that feeling, swallow it, absorb it and sweat it out the way he had, if only for one night on one beach.

I copied the definition of tremendous onto the final page of the notebook. I sucked Southern Comfort and spoke stumbling poetry to the darkening sky—for the writing gods and for

65

Kerouac, for the full moon, for hope, for words. I stripped to my paisley boxers and danced a silly jig around the fire, and I raised my bottle in a toast to Pat Kelly. Months before, in that drunken dawn at the kitchen table, I was reading from *On the Road*, and he stopped me when I said, "they danced down the streets like dingledodies."

He laughed and shook his head and pounded the table. He said, "Cousin, what in the blue fuck is a dingledodie?"

I tried to explain that Kerouac invented the word. I said, "You have to get the meaning from the story and the rhythm and the way the word sounds in your heart."

There was a pause during which Pat carefully refilled my shot glass with tequila. Then he stood up and stretched his upper body across the table so he was leaning on his elbows and his face was close and out of focus. He said, "What I want to know is, do you say more with all these words, or just talk more?"

I toasted him now from the sands of Summerland—and I toasted my father and Emmalita and Kerouac and Terry the All-American bum. Because words do make men. And women and toys and news and futures and lovers and wars, every question, every answer, the whole damn thing including the part we name our soul—the part that's invisible to our physical senses yet we feel it tremble at life. In the end what is the trembling made of, if not words?

I found my overalls rumpled on the sand. I slipped the postcard out of my pocket and looked at it with the firelight bouncing off the glossy photo. I turned it over and laughed at the joke one more time, then I tossed it into the flames and watched it catch fire. I pulled Terry's sunglasses out and threw them in as well. I ran to the backpack and grabbed the reporter's notebook. Page after page, word after word, I tore out and crumpled, and I offered them all to the giddy flames.

I slept straight through to the late morning sun like a man sated by exhaustion. I got up and walked into the ocean. All the sweat and dirt and doubt of the road rafted away on the foam. I finally caught a ride into Carpinteria that afternoon, Friday, a full week after I tromped up that first on-ramp in the fog of Stockton.

I found The Palms, and I found Pat there in a cramped little bar off the restaurant. Maybe six stools at the counter and a few tables in the corner, every spot filled with drinking, shouting, haranguing men. It was a workingman's bar. They were carpenters, painters, bricklayers and plumbers, and there was not a suit among them or a doubtful word. Down the bar there was some kind of contest taking place, and a huddle of men chanted and slammed their fists on the bar in unison. Of course Pat was in the middle of the commotion. I fished the last coins out of my pocket, ordered a draft and watched him in the bar back mirror.

He'd changed somehow. He was shirtless, that wasn't new. And he sat at the bar like a rooster, still chin up and shoulders back. But the hat was new—a dented straw cowboy hat the color of September hills, the brim rolled up a little on the sides, dirt blonde ponytail hanging out in the back. And the mustache was new—a trimmed biker-style Fu Manchu that added a thousand miles to his face. But he hadn't changed that much. The matronly woman who brought my beer told me he was eating raw cayenne peppers on a bet, with two more to go before winning the pile of money laid out in front of him. "Boys," she said, and shook her head.

Pat drained his mug in one swig and wiped his mouth with the back of a sun-dark arm. He looked down at the waxy red peppers in the clear glass snack bowl. He drew a deep breath and raised his right hand to the edge of the bowl. Then he spotted me in the mirror.

"Well, I'll be damned!" he hollered out, and he turned on his stool with a holy goof grin and stood up and cried out to the whole bar, "It's my little cousin!" He made it sound like an extra goddamn payday, and some of the men belly-laughed and cheered and lifted their drinks. He held up a finger that said just a second, turned back to the bar, and picked up both of the remaining peppers. He held them up for all to see and the crowd roared approval. Then he dropped the red peppers daintily into his upturned mouth.

His shoulders tensed. He worked his jaw. His forehead beaded sweat. His eyes bulged and watered and his open hand pounded the bar. He chewed and swallowed and gagged so his cheeks filled up like Dizzy Gillespie trumpeting high C. He gulped down someone else's beer and then bowed his head in concentration— or possibly a sinner's prayer. The crowd hushed. He raised his head, swept up all the money with one hand, punched at heaven and hollered, "Bartender! Drinks all around!" A tremendous cheer erupted like the end of a long bloody war.

I shouted and roared and drank deeply. I exulted.

68

AS ORDER OF THE WHORL

Kenton Yee

Words in a whorl
flow predictably and true
as they've no free will,
so please allow me to
restart the whorl
over-

As I was taking leaf to ants,
their salad for the year,
I stopped to see my aunt
who lived high up some stairs

Ants' salad for the year
I tucked in doorman's hand
as I approached the stairs
to see my high up aunt

Regretting tipped the leaf,
I cut for ants Aunt's cake
while whirling disbelief
my careless tipping mistake

Went down and fed the ants
and studied lepton particles
on student loans and grants
while sucking coffee Popsicles®

I mastered lepton particles,
wrote thesis in no time
while sucking coffee Popsicles®
and scrimping cents and dimes

I wrote my words of time
while doorman courted money
I lived on sense and dimes
while doorman dated honeys

After doorman married money,
he hired me ghost his chronicle
while doorman kissed his honey,
his cock-and-bull I wrote

I set aside my vote,
sanitized his beliefs
With praise for bull I wrote,
he tipped me back the leaf

Myself unclear to me,
I strolled beneath some trees
with browning tipped-back leaf
in search of self to see

I knelt beneath a tree
and held leaf up to see
I asked with innocence,
"What's your quintessence?"

The leaf pled senescence
and curled in money's way,
said, "You're not cognizant
of who you are today."

My rash reaction:
I let the leaf from hand
Per initial intention,
I fed the leaf to ants

and went to law school

and did the-thing-in-itself
on Sand Hill Road

and then Manhattan

During which time my aunt died
and nobody told me
and so I missed her funeral
as order of the whorl

To be as far this mourning
from the whorl as preceding
within it

The ants are antsy
(the leaves are leaping)
beneath the ukulele trees
to spin this whorl
over again

DARYL THE MAILMAN

Diane Byington

Daryl liked to wear his Elvis wig when he delivered the mail to his rural route, and in between mailboxes, he practiced for his gigs. He was trying to perfect the little catch in Elvis's voice, and he belted out the phrase, "Don't be cruel," over and over. The postal job itself was boring, but with the wig he didn't have to be Daryl the Mailman. He could be Daryl the Elvis Impersonator.

At the end of this day he noticed a text from Arturo, his supervisor. "Stop in and see me before you leave." Sighing, he wondered what he had done wrong. Back at the post office, Daryl stuffed the wig into his locker, tucked in his shirt, and ran his fingers through his mussed hair. He walked through the mostly-empty building, nodding at Carmen, another mail carrier.

"How's it going?" Carmen asked "Fine. I guess." He shrugged and rubbed his forehead, trying to rid himself of the headache that had started pounding when he received Arturo's text. He hadn't slept well recently, and he hated to see the expressions of sympathy on his colleagues' faces.

Arturo looked up when Daryl knocked at his office door. "There you are. Have a seat."

Daryl pursed his lips and sat. He hoped he wasn't going to get fired. It wasn't easy to fire a postal service employee, though, so that probably wasn't it. Still, something was seriously wrong.

Arturo was a few years younger than Daryl. Maybe forty. He'd shot up the hierarchy from mail carrier to station supervisor in record time. Outside the office he liked to party, but during work hours he was all business. Now he shook his head. "Mrs. Fernandez was in today. She pushed her walker into my office and waved the letter that you didn't pick up in my face. That's the second time this week. What's up?"

Oh, shit. Mrs. Fernandez lived nearly a quarter mile off of Highway 64 on a dirt road. She received so little mail that he sometimes forgot to check her mailbox. He couldn't tell his supervisor that he'd been too busy rehearsing to bother, so he opted to pass the blame. "If she would move her mailbox to the main road like everyone else, I wouldn't forget."

"You know we gave her a waiver. She's too frail to walk all the way to the main road, and she doesn't drive. This was her utility bill, and her power almost got shut off because of you. She had to get a neighbor to drive her in so she could deliver it."

Daryl's bravado seeped away. "Oh. I'm sorry. I'll do better."

"If you don't, I'll have to put you on report. Go by her house tomorrow and apologize. And, for God's sake, check her mailbox when you go."

"No problem. I really am sorry."

"Word is that the old lady is a *bruja*," Arturo said, and laughed. "You don't want to piss her off too much, or you might get turned into a toad."

Daryl thought a minute. He'd only been in Chama for a year. He might have heard that word before, but he wasn't sure. "*Bruja?*"

"Yeah. Some people say she's a healer, but others think she's a witch. I don't know if it's true, but you need to apologize to her. For a bunch of reasons."

"I already said I'd do it. Don't worry."

Arturo nodded, then closed his office door. "All right," he said, sitting back down. "Our conference is officially over. What's really going on?"

Daryl shook his head. "Nothing really. I'm a little jumpy about this gig I've got this weekend. It's the first one since Dolores left." He didn't mention that the divorce papers had arrived in yesterday's mail. If he didn't sign them right away, she might call to find out why. And then he could try and change her mind. But Dolores was unpredictable. He had to think about it some more.

"I know you enjoy being an Elvis impersonator," Arturo said.

"But you write good songs. Why don't you get a gig singing your own songs instead of impersonating some dead guy?"

"People like Elvis." Daryl remembered Dolores's biting words as she stormed out the door: "You drink too much. You have no personality. And you can't even sing Elvis right." He didn't disagree. He might not be able to develop a personality that Dolores would like, but if he could just perfect the little catch in his voice, at least he could do Elvis better.

"I think people would like you, too, if they got to know you."

They sat in silence for a few minutes. Finally, Arturo said, "You want to go get a beer or something? We should be able to get in at the High Country."

"Nah. I'm not drinking any more. Dolores doesn't like me when I'm drunk."

"Oh. Okay." He hesitated. "Have you heard from her lately?"

"No." The divorce papers had been from her lawyer, so he wasn't technically lying. "I'm hoping she'll come back if she hears I've stopped drinking."

For a moment, Arturo stared at him with a mixture of pity and tenderness. Then, in a lighter voice, he asked, "Where you playin' this weekend?"

"In a retirement community in Taos. They're celebrating the fiftieth wedding anniversaries of some of the residents. The old people like Elvis songs."

"Well, good luck with it. Hey, come in tomorrow afternoon and let me know how it goes with Mrs. Fernandez, okay?"

"Sure." Daryl trudged out of the office. His head ached and he really wanted a beer, but if he started drinking, he might not stop. Besides, he needed to rehearse.

The next morning, Daryl drove to Mrs. Fernandez's mobile home, tucked up against a tall cliff. There was no mail, either outgoing or incoming. He knocked on her door and, after a long moment, it swung open.

Mrs. Fernandez was gaunt, like she hadn't eaten in a while. The old woman held onto the door and swayed. Daryl wanted to grab her to keep her from falling, but he wasn't sure it would be appropriate. He waited, prepared to catch her if she fell. After a moment she said, "You're the mailman. The Elvis one."

"Yes, ma'am. I'm sorry I didn't pick up your mail yesterday."

The old woman frowned. "That's all right. I took care of it." She pointed inside and said, "Come in and sit for a few minutes. I haven't had a visitor recently."

Daryl was too busy to sit and visit, but he couldn't turn the old woman down. "Uh, okay. Just for a minute." He walked into the home, past the avocado green washer and dryer, past the cat dish with dried food stuck on the side, and into the living room, where a game show filled the giant TV screen. The sound was so loud that he nearly covered his ears, but he stopped himself in time. Even if he didn't have a personality, at least he could be polite.

Mrs. Fernandez clicked off the TV. The quiet was startling. Daryl sat on the edge of a faded blue recliner, and a grey cat jumped onto his lap. Mrs. Fernandez lowered herself onto a patched green sofa.

Looking around the room, Daryl noticed half a dozen African-type wooden masks hanging on the walls. He'd seen masks like these on "Antiques Roadshow," and, if he remembered correctly, they'd been worth a lot. A paper Lone Ranger-type mask was tacked to the wall behind the couch. *Strange*.

Daryl wanted to ask about the masks, but he forced himself to look at the old woman, who was staring at him with a twinkle in her eyes. He'd never been inside one of his customers' homes before. This one wasn't clean, but it was habitable. Maybe as clean as his own home, now that his wife wasn't around to remind him to clean it.

He cleared his throat. "Like I said, I'm sorry about missing you yesterday, and the other times, too. I'll do a better job of looking for your mail in the future."

Mrs. Fernandez nodded. "You might not believe this, but I was young once. I did a lot of things back then. Waitress. Cook. I liked being out and about." She looked at Daryl expectantly.

Daryl wondered what she wanted of him. With the exception of the masks on the wall, she seemed to be an ordinary old woman, almost like his grandmother back in Atlanta. He wouldn't have taken her for a famous witch. Or rather, *bruja*.

"That's great, ma'am. It's nice to be outside and not stuck behind a desk all the time. I like that, too." He hesitated, then started to rise. "Sorry I can't stay and visit. I've got to deliver other people's mail." The cat tumbled off his lap. "I can let myself out," he said. "No need for you to get up." He walked to the sofa and reached down to shake her hand. "Nice meeting you, ma'am. Have a good day."

A streak of lighting ran up his arm when their hands touched. "What the…" He immediately jerked his hand away and shook

78

it, trying to get the feeling back.

Mrs. Fernandez pulled herself to a standing position. "What's wrong, son? Can I help you?"

"I … something happened when we shook hands. A shock or something."

The old woman frowned. "I wonder if that was because of my heart defibrillator. It sometimes goes off and shocks me, but I've never known it to shock another person. I'm sorry if I hurt you."

The trailer's floor seemed to roll under Daryl's feet. He needed to get out of there, quick. "Uh, no problem. See you later." He moved toward the door.

"Wait a minute, mijo," she said. "I've got something for you." She pushed her walker into the kitchen. Reaching into an upper cupboard, she pulled down a plastic bag filled with something that looked like dried weeds, then poured a portion of it into a brown paper bag. She turned to Daryl. "Here. Try this for a few days. It might help you."

"No thank you, ma'am. My arm's getting better already." But it wasn't. It felt numb all the way up to his shoulder.

She nodded like she understood he was lying but didn't want to call him on it. "I didn't mean to hurt you. But this will help."

Trying to look grateful, he took the bag. "Uh, what is it?"

"Tea. After you boil a cup of water, put in one tablespoon of this and let it steep for ten minutes. Then drink it. It'll make you feel better."

"Thank you." He turned to leave.

"And come back in a week and let me know how it worked."

She laughed. It wasn't exactly a witchy cackle. But close.

Outside, he breathed a sigh of relief and got into his truck. There was no way he was going to drink that tea or come back to see that old lady. She might or might not be a *bruja*. One thing was certain, though. He would never again forget to pick up her mail.

The numbness in his arm receded as the afternoon wore on. He wished he had someone to tell about the strange encounter. If his wife had been home, he would have told her. Back at the post office, he knocked at Arturo's door. His supervisor waved him inside. "How did it go?"

"Your frail little old lady just tried to kill me. She shocked the shit out of me when we shook hands. My arm still feels strange."

"What?"

When Daryl finished telling the story, Arturo shook his head. "I think maybe she was playing one of her tricks on you. She's kind of famous for them. I'm glad you're okay. Strange things happen back in these hills, my friend. Land of Enchantment and all that. You're not in Georgia anymore."

"I'm okay. Hey, you want to go to the park to watch the sunset?"

The next Saturday night, after Daryl had sung all his Elvis songs and received a standing ovation for "Don't Be Cruel," he took a deep breath and said, "I wrote this one. Hope you enjoy it."

He'd written the sad song a few weeks before. Deep love and loss were his realities, and the words reflected his longing for his wife. To his ears, he sounded like a lonesome wolf howling in the desert. When he finished, the applause was scattered. A few people cried. Others seemed confused.

This had been a disaster. He should have chosen a more upbeat song. But he didn't have any of those. So he ended with a fast Elvis song, and everyone seemed relieved.

He didn't know why he'd tried out one of his songs on this group. Maybe it was because of the pretty activities director who smiled at him from the corner of the room. He wanted her to think of him as more than a guy in a greasy black wig and a sparkling suit. He looked for her after his last song, but she was nowhere to be seen.

"Figures," he thought. "People would rather have Elvis than Daryl. I knew it all along."

On Sunday evening, his phone rang. Dolores, at last. He tried to keep from sounding too eager when he answered.

"I just called to tell you that I'm getting married again," she said. "Have you signed the papers yet?"

Married? She'd only been gone for five weeks. And they'd been together for eight years. "I don't understand. We're not even divorced yet."

"So what?"

Leaving his computer programming job in Atlanta and moving to New Mexico hadn't been enough to sustain their marriage, then. He tried to think what to say, then asked, "Uh, do I know him?"

"No, you don't know him. I'm livin' in Denver now. How many people do you know in Denver?"

"None."

"All right, then."

He paused. "I stopped drinking after you left."

"That's good. But it wasn't just the drinking that made me leave. It plain didn't work between us, Daryl. We're different people, is all. I know you moved to Chama to help me take care of Mama, but she's dead now. I couldn't stay there. You don't have to, either."

"I'll move to Denver if you want me to."

"How many times do I have to tell you?" Her irritation was loud and clear. "It's over with us. You need to move on with your life. I have."

He sighed. "All right. I'll give the papers to my lawyer and see what he says."

Dolores snorted, like she knew he didn't have a lawyer. "You do that."

After they hung up, he stared at the phone for a long while. Then he went out to the garage and tinkered with his motorcycle. Later, he drove to the liquor store and bought a fifth of vodka. Back home, he set the bottle on the counter and stared at it. He wanted to drink the whole thing at one sitting. Drink until he passed out on the floor. If he inhaled his own vomit and died, so be it.

He fingered the one-month chip from AA that he kept in his pocket.

He stared at that bottle for a long, long time. Then he noticed the bag of tea Mrs. Fernandez had given him. He'd dropped it onto the counter when he'd gotten home that day and hadn't thought about it since. A voice in his head said: *Why not try it?*

His arm turned numb just as it had when he had shaken her hand. To distract himself, he brewed up the tea and took a sip. It tasted like the chamomile tea his mother had given him when he had an upset stomach. Strange to taste it now, so many years later. He added honey and drank the entire cup. It warmed his heart as well as his stomach. And it seemed to ease the headache that had been his constant companion for weeks.

When he went to bed, the bottle still sat on the counter, unopened, and he felt a little better.

At work the next day, instead of playing Elvis songs in his truck, he played an old recording by Leonard Cohen. His favorite song was "Suzanne." His first girlfriend had been named Suzy, and he wondered what had happened to her.

The day was one of the most beautiful he could remember. Aspen trees quaked in a light breeze and sent their orange and yellow leaves drifting onto his truck. Snow might arrive later in the evening. Even if things weren't working out for him at the moment, he was still glad he'd moved here.

Mrs. Fernandez's front door was closed, and there was no mail, in or out. He hoped the old lady was all right, but he didn't stop. She'd probably forgotten that she'd asked him to return.

He found a check in his mailbox from the retirement home. The activities director had included a note with the check. "Thank you for your concert last Saturday. The residents particularly loved that sad song you played near the end. At least half a dozen people have asked me to get you back to sing more songs like that. They like Elvis, but that song really spoke to them. What do you think?"

She'd signed the note, "Suzanne." Strange. He hadn't known her name.

He drank another cup of tea. The next day he took the vodka to work and handed the bottle to Arturo, who smiled and nodded his thanks.

Every evening during the next week, Daryl wrote down songs as they drifted by. He signed the divorce papers and sent them back. His colleagues started smiling at him without sympathy in their eyes.

The next Saturday night he returned to the retirement home and sang his own songs. Although they were all sad, he discovered that his well of sadness wasn't as deep as it had been. People clapped hard after every song, often with tears in their eyes. By the end of the concert, he knew his days as an Elvis impersonator were over.

Suzanne thanked him and walked him to his car. He took a deep breath before speaking. "I come to Taos pretty often. Would you like to get a cup of coffee or something the next time I'm in town?"

She smiled. "Yes."

On Monday, he stopped at Mrs. Fernandez's house. When he knocked at her door, the woman who answered appeared younger than before. She didn't use a walker, and didn't sway like she was off-balance. But she was the same woman, Daryl thought, just younger. What the...?

"Come in, come in. It's nice to see you again."

The trailer was clean and tidy. The cat bowl was newly

washed, dishes were clean and stacked in the drainer, and the television was off. Daryl gulped. How could the old woman have changed so much in such a short time? He didn't ask, just handed her a letter from someone in New Orleans.

"Thank you," she said. "Sit down, please. Could I get you some tea?"

"Uh, no thanks, ma'am. I just came to thank you for the tea you gave me before. It sure helped me. I wonder … could I ask what was in it?"

"As I recall, it was chamomile. I picked it myself." She gestured to a small garden outside the trailer.

"Chamomile? Just chamomile? Nothing, uh, special?"

She laughed. This time it sounded like the tinkle of a music box. "No, nothing special. You've probably heard the rumors about me. Not true. I'm just a former waitress who lives alone since my husband died. I don't want anybody breaking in, so I allow those rumors to persist."

He had no idea what to say to that. They sat for a while in silence. Finally, she asked, "What's that you're holding?"

He bit his lip, wondering whether he was being foolish. Finally, he decided to go for it. Hoping she wouldn't be offended, he said, "Uh, ma'am, it's the Elvis wig I used to wear. I don't have a need for it anymore. I know it's silly, and feel free to say no, but I wondered if you would want it. You know, for your wall. It's not a mask, I know, but it seems to fit with the others."

She looked up at the wall and nodded. "Thank you, son. It will have its own special place." She took the wig from him and patted it.

As he stood to leave, she asked, "*Mijo*, would you like some more tea?"

"No, I don't think so," he said. "I appreciate it, though."

Soon after, he requested a transfer to Taos. The next year, after their marriage, he told Suzanne the story about Mrs. Fernandez. They drove up on his motorcycle to visit her.

When they arrived, the mobile home was deserted, with tall weeds growing around it and clumps of animal scat in the driveway. The mailbox had been torn down. Daryl parked, and he and Suzanne walked up to the front door. It was open, so they went inside. All of the furniture was gone. No washer or dryer, no cat bowl, no couch or chair, no TV. And no masks on the wall.

Daryl went into the kitchen and opened the upper cupboard. Inside was a brown paper bag filled with something that looked like weeds. The words, "Daryl the Mailman," were written on the side. He pulled down the bag and held it up to his nose. Chamomile tea. It smelled fresh.

"How did she know we were coming?" asked Suzanne, a tone of wonder in her voice. "Do you think she moved down the street or something, and saw us drive up?"

He shrugged. "I don't know. Why don't we ask her neighbor?"

They walked the quarter mile to the next house. Daryl knocked, and a middle-aged woman answered the door.

"Hello," she said. "May I help you?"

Daryl cleared his throat. "I was wondering about Mrs. Fernandez, who used to live down the road. Do you know what happened to her?"

The woman nodded. "Oh, yes. She moved to New Orleans to live with her sister. I correspond with her from time to time. She seems to like it there." She glanced at the bag in Daryl's hands. "Ah, it looks like you've been to the trailer. Did she leave that for you?"

"I ... I guess so," Daryl said. "But it looks like it was put there recently. I don't know what to think."

The woman was quiet for a moment. "Mrs. Fernandez is a powerful shaman. Her ways of healing people are ... unique, I guess I would say. I wouldn't ask too many questions, if I were you. Just accept the gift and use it when you need it." She peered at him. "Have I seen you before? You look familiar."

"I used to be your mailman."

"Ah. Mrs. Fernandez spoke of you often. You were one of her favorites."

"Favorites?"

Suzanne and Daryl looked at each other, not knowing what to say. Finally, the woman asked, "Would you like her forwarding address?"

Daryl nodded, then accepted the piece of paper she handed him. "*Buena suerte,*" she said, closing the door.

He and Suzanne planned to take a trip to Atlanta next summer. After they spent some time with his family, he might suggest they take a couple of extra days and drive over to New Orleans. He'd like to see if his friend was displaying his Elvis wig on her wall.

STIRRING THE POT

Victoria Grant

I.

Betty stirred the pot of rice in a slow, circular motion, reaching deep into the creases for every grain. The scraping of the wooden spoon against the sides and bottom of the pot rasped a steady tempo. Her tall frame swayed with the motion of her arm, almost as if tuned in to some semblance of exotic music made up of the resonances of wood and metal.

She'd married at nineteen because Henry Clarke had chosen her, even though he could have had most any girl he wanted.

Athletically built, easy on the eyes, and boasting of a promising desk job career at a computer firm, Henry was an ideal husband for any questing woman. Smooth-talking, love-to-love, need-to-be-me Henry rejected everyone else for the quiet little girl in the corner.

Betty's eyes strayed to the clock. Six-fifteen. Henry would be home soon enough. Her nerves tightened, and she lost the rhythm. Now she thought only to offer a properly cooked pot of rice, one that he wouldn't condemn as tasteless mush or pebbly grit.

In the undersized pantry of the peaches and cream kitchen barely brightened by natural light through the room's frosted window, she kept a 50-pound bag (thank the stars for Costco) of special-grown, Carolina long-grain rice. With no written instructions, she tried learning the skill of cooking this rice observing Henry's mother. Though they'd lived with Mrs. Clarke the first six months of their married life, Betty hadn't been given one bit of helpful advice. Mrs. Clarke didn't use precise measurements. How much water? How much salt? How much rice? How long to let the rice boil hard before simmering? The six-foot-tall, condescending matriarch of the family would only say, "Pay attention and you'll learn." Betty had been trying to get it right, but failing, for months. Henry acted out with escalating signs of impatience.

Henry's mother brooked no back-talk from her adult sons and daughters – and definitely not from the inadequate daughter-in-law. She made clear she was not impressed with Betty's efforts to help around the house. Offers to assist with meals: rejected.

Menial cleaning tasks: sort of accepted, as the results were always judged "not quite right," and needed Mrs. Clarke's personal touch-ups. Betty thought it best to follow the ways of Henry and his siblings: she accepted Mrs. Clarke's scorn quietly.

The first few weeks, pleas to Henry to move to their own place were dismissed with, "Don't sweat the small stuff, baby, we'll move soon enough." Around the fourth month, his response had been to shove her away, hard. "Woman, what's your problem, why you acting so stupid? You doing well enough here, so don't start stuff where there ain't none."

His dismissive reactions hurt her feelings, if not her body. Why was she failing to keep her husband happy? Her own mother never instructed her in the ways of being a "proper" wife. So Betty studied *Home* magazine and fifties-TV family sitcoms, the ones with the most obedient wives, like *Father Knows Best, Leave it to Beaver,* or *The Donna Reed Show.* Message received: To be happy and worthy, it's a wife's duty to satisfy her husband. Henry said, "Don't question my judgment." She obeyed.

Once or twice, she tried broaching the subject to her parents, but verbalizing the situation made her feel foolish. Mom said, "Aren't you being a little oversensitive? For Pete's sake, he's not killing you." Poppie said, "You made your bed, lie in it," followed with the rebuke, "And stop putting your business out in the street." Anyway, as her friend Marsha would declare, "Shyst happens." Okay.

Mrs. Clarke called them to her living room one evening, and said, "Henry, your baby sister, Callie, is finished with that no-good man she married. She's coming back here with the babies, so we're going to need you two's room. Time you got your own place. I talked to Cousin Etta, and she's got a rental for you."

A week later, Betty was happily decorating their one-bedroom cottage. She chose earth-tone Ikea-like furnishings, and arranged on the bed and sofa some colorful Moroccan-designed pillows. Henry had difficulties getting over being "thrown out" of his own home. She tried settling his moods by cooking the dishes that she watched his mother prepare. Henry's usual complaint: "The rice ain't right."

Though she told herself stressing over that one failure was irrational – the inability to make a perfect pot of rice – the shortcoming now marked her wifely qualifications, and stood high and above the many others Henry chose to point out. It didn't help that on weekdays rice was the only side-dish he would allow. Henry wouldn't tolerate anything else. His mother did it, why couldn't she? He didn't seem to think much of whatever she did was right, so she wanted to do this one thing to his satisfaction.

Tonight he refused to eat his meal, and flung the plate at her. "Bitch, what's this crap?" The plate of two onion and gravy smothered pork chops with sides of spicy collard greens and steaming pearl white rice slid down her own peaches and cream colored wall, dragging her heart with it.

II.

The glazed russet brown of the baked chicken contrasted against the dull black of the cast iron Dutch oven. Caramelized onions, peppers, carrots and string beans surrounded the perfect bird. No potatoes. Weekdays were for the consumption of rice only; Henry wouldn't have it any other way. Betty turned down the oven to Warm. Now she would concentrate on just cooking the rice. Try again to get it right.

She swiped a profusion of sweat from her forehead with the back of her hand. She ran water in the pot to a line scratched in three inches below the rim, then set the range fire to High. The palms of her hands were moist, and she rubbed them down the front of her jeans to dry.

At Marsha's coded knock on the door, a slight frown creased Betty's forehead. "Damn, Marsha, not now," she whispered, but the childhood friend poked her healthy round face through the doorway.

"Betty, I know you don't like me coming this late in the day, but I couldn't pass by without saying Hey." Marsha loped long strides across the kitchen, stripped off her pea coat, and tossed it onto the back of a chair. She opened the cupboard over the kitchen sink and snatched the I-heart-New York oversized mug off the shelf.

"Oh! Wait! There's a chip in that one," Betty said. "Let me give you a better one."

"No way!" Marsha said.

Betty stared at the miniscule chip on the bottom, knowing Henry would totally lose it if he spied the flaw. A further example of her housewife imperfection.

"I'm saving its life. It needs love," Marsha said, flashing one of her persistent gap-toothed smiles. She plucked a tea bag out the tin can, dropped it into the cold water, and slipped the rescued mug into the microwave.

Betty knew she would begin chatting away once the microwave zapped her tea. "Marsha, I need you to cooperate with me. Go over there and sit quietly to drink your tea. I got to do this thing right," she pleaded.

Marsha didn't blink. She walked up to inspect the pot of water on the stove, the box of salt, and measuring cup of rice on the counter. "Can I ask you something?"

Betty caved. "Of course, Marsha, anything." The salted water was boiling. Time to add the rice.

"Well, I don't want to get into your business, or anything."

"You're my best friend, you know you can ask me anything."

"Well, I used to know, but lately . . . ever since you got married, and all . . ."

"What? What does my getting married have to do with anything?"

Marsha twisted her bottom lip. The microwave buzzed. She retrieved the mug and carefully sipped the black chai while Betty poured a bit of salt, then the measured rice into the water. They sat in tense silence while Betty slowly stirred the pot of rice. She looked up. Her smile slowly lifted her firm cheeks, squinting her eyes.

Betty noted, however, the pupils projected like scintillating jewels through the slits. She took a deep breath and smiled along with Marsha. "What d'you want to ask me, brat?"

Marsha laughed. "Who you calling a brat? You a married lady all of a year, and you think you all that."

Betty returned her attentions to the rice.

"I got news for you, girl, you all tied up in knots. You looking tired, too, with them bags under your eyes, and stuff. If being married does all that, I may have to think twice about marrying my man for a while yet. Anyway, I wasn't trying to bother you, I just wanted to ask why you always cooking rice? Don't Henry ever eat anything else?"

"Of course he does, but he likes rice. So I try to fix it for him like Mother d---"

Marsha broke in. "Mother? Whose Mother?"

"Henry's mother. That's what he calls her, and he wants me to call her that, too." Betty glanced over at Marsha who was covering her mouth from the sputtering laughter.

"Oh, Betty, I'm sorry," Marsha said after she had regained her composure. "I really am. Only I suddenly got this image of you as this oh-so-proper stuck-up. I mean, really Betty. Mother? Oh Blessed Lord, the silly pretense."

Marsha's laugh was contagious. The laughter lasted way too long, but Betty couldn't easily let go of this rare, carefree moment. Then she shot a glance up at the clock, and shut down as sudden as a slammed door.

"Marsha, listen, I hate to rush you, but you gotta go. I still have this cooking to finish, and Henry will be leaving his office for home soon." That anxious wheedling had returned to her voice.

Marsha got up, tossed the teabag in the trash, rinsed her mug out in the sink and stashed it in the dishwasher. She turned to Betty, reached out, and placed both hands on her shoulders.

Betty flinched.

Marsha dropped her arms and stepped – almost jumped –

back. "What's wrong?"

Betty felt a gut-wrenching guilt. This was her best friend, and she didn't like holding back. Nevertheless, she was married, and she owed loyalty to her husband. Her throat tightened.

Marsha turned away and retrieved her pea coat. Shoving her arms into the sleeves, she walked slowly towards the door. Just before leaving, she looked over her shoulder. "Bets?"

Betty was undone by her friend's soft tone. She gazed down into the sink and leaned on it for strength. No emotional vitality remained to even glance up at her friend. There was nothing she would share.

"We're BFF, girlfriend. I mean it, best friends for-ev-er." Marsha said. "We declared that from the time we first met in kindergarten, and we promised it again in the church's dressing room before I lifted the ends of that hellified long wedding gown train of yours down the aisle. Don't you ever forget any of that."

Betty could only nod her lowered head.

"Okay, well, I'm outta here. I'll call later in the week."

Betty fixed hard on to her friend's eyes. "You promise?"

Marsha walked back across the kitchen to air-kiss both Betty's cheeks. "Girl, go on back to that stove, and take care of your husband. I'll call you Thursday or Friday. One day I'm going to sit down with you two and find out what's so special about that damn rice." She flipped a tender wave at Betty, and her "*Ciao*" floated on the aroma of boiling, special-grown, Carolina long-grain rice.

Betty feared losing her. Henry disliked her friends and didn't mind letting them know. The friends dwindled away. Except for Marsha, who basically ignored his rudeness and taunting comments ("As long as he doesn't lay a finger on me, we're good.").

She turned back to stirring the pot – and wondered what flavor the rice would take on with her teardrops stirred into the grains.

III.

Betty stirred the pot of rice while thinking about the passage of years since Marsha and her family had been over to dinner. Sure, they caught-up on phone calls now and then, but growing kids, after-school programs, marital responsibilities, and just plain busywork got in the way of real visits. It had taken one of Henry's computer programs to synchronize all their schedules. She smiled when she thought of his promotion to Director. A congratulatory dinner was as good excuse as any for the two families to get together.

The increased salary was a blessing, easing the burden of the larger mortgage for the new house. Betty was still doubtful they needed a house this huge. Seventy-five hundred square feet, a media center, six bedrooms, four and a half bathrooms. And, Good Lord, a guest cottage. They only had two kids, and no one from his family ever stayed overnight, not even Henry's mom . . . er, not even Mother. Didn't people call these residential monstrosities McMansions?

"We finally live in the right zip code," he said. "That's what my clients will like. Trust me, babe, believe in what I'm doing."

Betty didn't feel like stirring the pot of rice, but she did it anyway. Performing this ritual kept Henry off her back, and it kept the peace. She lifted the spoon into the air for a moment. The word "peace" stuck in her mind, hanging in the air as if in a gravity-free container. What is peace, Betty wondered? She didn't believe her home ever saw a day of it. Not in twenty years.

Marsha tapped their coded knock on the kitchen island behind Betty, whose spirits reawakened to hear that friendly call.

"Hey, lady, we're all here and accounted for."

Betty felt an unfamiliar grin sweeping across her face. "Ha! That diet and exercise working for you, girlfriend."

Marsha spun around ballet-like, modeling a red-on-white spaghetti-strapped sundress. "You like?" Then she threw up her bare arms in a mock bodybuilder pose, framing the still-full face with the ever-ready gap-toothed smile. "I'm going to stay twenty-nine the rest of my life."

Not breaking the stirring motion, Betty jutted out a cheek for Marsha's air-kiss. "You look it – even though you're thirty-five. I hate you.

Now make yourselves comfortable, while I finish up this rice, and . . ."

Running into the kitchen, her twelve-year-old son interrupted her. Tall for his age, slim build, and sinewy muscles protruding from the sleeveless T-shirt that supported impressive skills on the basketball court, Mikey's facial features also revealed his father's Cherokee heritage. He'd also acquired his father's foul temper. "Mom, where's my X-box game? That one I was playing with last night, I can't find it. Where'd you put it? Give it to me, I need it."

"Mikey! You see Miss Marsha here. Mind your manners, and say Hello."

"I know she's here," he said, as if he wanted to add "Stupid" to the end of his statement. "Why d'ya think I want the game? I wanna play it with Gary." Again, the slightest pause for the unsaid insult.

"Mikey . . ."

"Why can't you just do what I ask you to do?" Mikey shouted, then stalked out of the kitchen.

Marsha stared at Betty. "What's going on here?"

Betty turned her back, covered the pot of rice leaving an opened slit for venting, and turned down the heat. "I guess the rice is ruined now," she said softly to herself. A fleeting glance at her watch. "Should I start another pot?"

"Bets, talk to me. Why's Mikey acting like that? I swear, if Gary ever dreamed of talking at me like that, he'd find himself coming up off the floor. Not even my husband talks to me like that. How could you take that kind of behavior from him?"

"It's complicated, Marsha," Betty said, tugging at the cuffs of her long sleeves. "Mikey kind of seen some things that's made him a little angry at me."

"A little," yelped Marsha. "Betty, that was total disrespect I just witnessed. And I'm getting very bad vibes that scene was only the tip of the proverbial iceberg." Marsha drew her gaze down the length of her friend's long sleeves.

Just then, Mikey's younger sister, Lizzie, ran crying into Betty's arms. "Mommy, Mikey's hitting me again, make him go away. I don't know where his old game is."

Betty yelled out, "Mikey, bring your narrow behind back in here."

Mikey dragged his feet into the kitchen, face displaying a sulky glare. "What?"

"I've just about had enough from you," Betty said in a scorching tone. "You apologize to your sister and straighten out your act today, I mean right now, or your little butt is going to catch a mean whipping."

Mikey gave Betty a savage look. "You touch me, and I'll tell Dad. Then we'll see whose butt gets whipped." He produced a wicked smile. "He'll beat your behind, not mine." He jammed his hands into his pants pockets, turned on a heel, and, rolling his shoulders into each step, sauntered out the room.

Marsha stammered, "I can't believe this. If you don't tell me what's happening, I swear—"

Betty raised a stiff-armed hand in the internationally recognized signal for Stop. "Don't! This is a family issue, Marsha. I'll deal with it. Let it be." She caught Marsha staring at her wrist, and realized the edge of the purplish bruise peeked out. Her arm buckled and dropped. From the depths of her soul, manifested through rage-filled, saddened eyes, she begged, "Please . . . Let. It. Be."

A LETTER OF LOVE

Meg Serino

We are on the boat—a yacht, you would correct me—the four of us. It is perfect. Gleaming white and shining silver. I slip my toes into the water's silk and am utterly alone. Lowering my hips, I stretch my arms as wide as the ocean, fingers reaching, searching. The water cools the heat of my sunbaked skin; my chin skims along the surface, dipping. I breathe in, close my eyes, plunge under. The chilled shock of silence. Of bathed oblivion. Of perfection.

"Deena," I hear my name called, echoing even under water. It pierces my watery cocoon, stilling me. "Lunch is ready—Deena!"

I bob to the surface. Smile.

Laura leans over the guardrails, motioning to me. "Cocktail?" Her teeth flash white; her teal and pink sundress flutters in the breeze.

"Yes!" I smile more broadly, swimming with my head above the water. I can see you and Dave sitting at the table on the deck. What I can't see I already know from the past five days, from the last eleven years that we've vacationed together like this, children and work and worries all left behind: in front of you is a drink—your second or third beer and the same number of vodka-on-the-rocks-with-a-twist for Dave; there is a bowl of salted nuts and a plate of assorted salamis and prosciutto, a selection of cheeses—no crackers or bread—and a platter of sliced fresh fruit, including figs, my favorite; later, an avocado and tomato salad will appear along with some grilled fish. It is our winter respite, our annual sunshine solution to the drabness of our days and our skin. Not that I'm complaining of life at home—really I'm not—my problems, as you say, lodge me between a pillow and a pillow. I know I'm lucky.

I swim up to the stern where the group sits, drinking and laughing. I can hear the clink of ice cubes in Dave's drink, the clatter of a knife against a plate. You will remember this part. Or maybe not: as I step onto the boat my heel slides out and I slip, ugly, my hands flailing, grasping, the inside of my left ankle and instep slicing open on one of the metal cleats that bedeck the stern on either side. I land hard on my right knee, panting, eyes stinging. Laura rushes over.

"Oh my God, honey, are you okay?" She bends down and

takes me by my elbows, raising me up. She puts her arm around my shoulder. Like I'm one of her kids when they were little: a scraped knee from skateboarding, a cracked clavicle from sledding.

I sit on the floor, staring dumbly at my ankle, the blood twirling down my leg in rivulets.

"I'll get the captain," Dave says, putting down his glass. He strides to the bow of the boat, all business, with purpose.

You walk towards me, holding your beer. "And you haven't even started drinking yet!" you chuckle, not unkindly, shaking your head. "What happened? What did you do?"

"Come on, let's get you more comfortable," Laura walks me over to the L-shaped cushioned seats that surround the table, holding onto me as if I'm some oddly shaped but fragile package.

"I'm okay," I say. "I'm fine. Really." Blood pools around my foot onto the deck.

"Geez, that's a lot of blood," you say. "Is that okay? Blood on the deck?"

I turn to look at you. You with the clear blue eyes. The easy gaze.

"It's fine," Laura says, grabbing a white cloth napkin from the table and pressing it to the wound.

I wince.

"I'm sorry hon," she says.

Dave returns, the captain in tow.

"So, what have we here?" Captain Dick asks. Remember how we laughed about his name when we first came on board? Our eyes met, hysterically, and yet it was only when we were safely in our cabin that we burst out in relief, hands clamped over open mouths, eyes tearing, the safety valve open for once and running free.

"It's nothing," I say. "It looks worse than it is."

"It looks pretty bad," Dave says. "Is there a first-aid kit aboard?"

"Do you think she needs stitches?" asks Laura.

"No," I say. "I'm sure it's fine."

Captain Dick bends down. "Let's have a look." He puts his hands gently over mine, which is pressing the napkin against the gash along my ankle. "Let me see." His voice is deep, soothing.

"Here," Dave says, handing me a drink. It's a Dark and Stormy, the mahogany rum swirling on top like a tiny tornado in a glass. "Chugalug. You've earned it."

You're standing next to me and then go over to the bar, taking another beer from the small refrigerator, stocked with mixers and limes, beer and wine. Popping off the top, you begin to search in several drawers for something, which you find, triumphant. You hold a jar aloft: more nuts. You smile. From here I can see the scar that runs a half-inch from the corner of your mouth to your chin where Bobby nicked you with his hoe; it glows whitely against your tanned skin. You never believed me how guilty he felt afterwards—he cried and cried as I was putting him to bed that night—he was only eight. His dark eyes huge in his little face. It was an accident. Not, as you always supposed, that he heard us arguing and was defending me. I can see you shaking your head, waving me off as you do, dismissing what I have to say as rubbish. Dismissing my words with a flutter of your fingers.

Captain Dick removes the napkin, holding my ankle. His hands are broad, large, with pronounced knuckles. "I'll be right back." I watch him stand, squinting against the sunlight reflecting off the water, the chrome of the guardrails. His tall, still-lean body retreats inside. I notice, not for the first time, that he walks with a limp.

When he returns, he is carrying a red medical kit.

"Captain Dick to the rescue!" you say, sitting down and resting your feet on the seat next to me. "Want one?" You set down the jar of nuts, taking one. You nod towards my ankle. "That's a lot of blood."

"I know, right?" Laura chimes in. "Like when Eric tripped on the curb and knocked his front teeth back into his gums when he was, what, three? All that blood! You couldn't even speak in the emergency room," she says to me. "Remember? You made me give them all the information—"

I grimace and sip my drink, savoring the bite of ginger beer, the burn of rum. The ice bumps into my upper lip, wetting it.

"Finish that, and I'll get you another," Dave says. "And you too." He winks at Laura. "I haven't forgotten about you."

"So he says now," Laura smiles wryly at her husband.

She sits next to me, on the side not occupied by your feet, as Captain Dick takes out a brown bottle of Betadine and some gauze. He kneels down and gets to work, talking as he swabs at the wound, asking me if it hurts, whether I've had a Tetanus shot recently, what we'd like to do for dinner tonight, our last night.

My ankle, my whole foot is on fire.

"We're going to catch dinner," Dave says. "Right? Our fishing

104

charter's at one."

"Count me out," I say, watching Captain Dick wrap my ankle and foot in gauze. His touch is firm but also light, just the right amount of pressure. "I think I'll stay put."

"Do you want me to stay?" asks Laura. Her eyes are large and light brown flecked with cinnamon; her brow unlined from a recent Botox injection. And by the way, just so you know: a smooth brow is not natural in women our age. "I don't mind, really, you know it's not like I care about fishing."

"Everyone should go," I say. "In fact, isn't it almost time?" Laura begins to shake her head. I continue, "No seriously, I'll feel terrible if I ruin everyone's plans. I mean it. Go." Captain Dick tapes the gauze in place, puts his supplies away and then stands.

"I'll have the steward bring you over in the dinghy," he says to the group. "It'll take just a few minutes."

"Are you sure?" you ask me. "You're not going to be mad at me about this later, are you?"

A small twist of anger flares in my chest. "Of course not." I wave them all off. "I'm going to be fine—I want to finish my book anyway—go have fun."

I hear the dinghy, roar off and then I'm alone. But not lonely. You never understood that difference. The ache of loneliness is deepest in the presence of someone you love. Alone, and the possibility for connection isn't possible; only failed possibility causes pain. What if I had asked you to stay? To forgo the high-pitched hum of casting a line; the flash of fish scales rainbowed by the sun; water droplets winging towards your baseball cap as a hooked fish swings onboard. The beer-soaked laughter. Backslaps. Handshakes. To keep me company instead, just the two of us.

I picture us stranded on separate decks: me in the sun, you in the shade.

Slowly, I hobble towards the bow where I can stretch out in the sun. Holding onto the railing, I pull myself along, realizing that my book is in the cabin below and I lack both the grace and energy to manage the stairs on my own.

No matter. I make myself comfortable on the white cushions that line the deck. Closing my eyes, I let the sun burn orange against my lids, let my thoughts lift and swirl with the breeze that catches my hair.

"Deena?"

It's Captain Dick. Even as I write his name it makes me smile—how immature I am!—although when I heard his voice then I smiled too. But differently.

I open my eyes and he stands next to me, holding a drink.

"Iced tea," he says. The glass drips perspiration.

"Thank you." I sit up, taking the glass from his outstretched hand. I notice the veins running along his arm; how the short sleeves of his shirt stretch taught against his biceps. His duties do not usually include serving drinks.

"How's your ankle?" he asks. "That's a deep cut you know, you're actually pretty lucky."

"I'm a spaz." I laugh. And you would agree: I'm always tripping or banging my knee or burning myself in the kitchen. "But I'm fine—and thanks for mopping me up—it probably isn't one of you typical duties. Sorry to be so much trouble."

"Not at all," he says. "You just needed a little tending to, that's all."

I nod, my throat aching in a way that makes it impossible for me to speak.

"Let me know if you want anything, okay?" He turns to leave. "Anything at all."

I open my mouth. I will the words to march out, in neat ordered rows, down my tongue and out into the space that separates us. I could cry I want to speak so.

As if he's heard me, he turns back. "Deena." He takes a step towards me.

He has heard me.

"I hope it's okay I say this—"

I nod again, my mouth—I am sure—still open.

And then he strides over, three great strides, and the heat of his mouth is pressing into mine, swallowing me in a swirl of salted blackness. In the white hot glare of the sun. The smell of sweat and soap and longing. His rough hands slide under me, arms wrap around me; the ache, a low tug, insistent—

"Deena?"

Dick is standing, as he was, across the deck. "—Is it too much sun on you? Would you like me to put down the awning?" He takes another step towards me. "You don't want to get burned on your last day."

I close my mouth. Shame burns my cheeks.

"No, thanks." The cotton-dry words are thick, clumsy. "I love

107

the sun."

"Me too," he says. "I can't take the cold. I don't know how you manage up North. All that snow."

And so I ask you: how do we manage?

For our last dinner we're seated around the white-clothed table, the silver winking with moonlight, the wineglasses already filled and then refilled with a cabernet so rich and dense I want to chew it. I wear a long white dress with spaghetti straps and a slit down the middle, revealing my still-slender legs, my narrow feet tucked into a pair of high-heeled mules, wrapped ankle be damned.

Did you notice? Do you know how hard I work to stay slim?

"You look gorgeous," I say to Laura, who is adjusting the halter-top of her dress. The outline of her nipples shows through its thin material; the silicone in her breasts bounces pleasingly as she lowers her arms.

I've seen your eyes graze those nipples. Don't bother denying it, not even in your head. And not just hers, either. What do you do on those business trips—those nights away from home— freed from the marital noose? When the boys were small and you were gone, we ate French toast for dinner and snuggled into bed, ankles and elbows and knees poking, wondrously, sandwiching in. And now that they're mostly gone, well, I'm alone. And you?

Before dinner Laura asked me about Captain Dick, although she anointed him with a different title, which I'll spare you.

"What about him?" I said. We were sitting on the deck watching the sunset, its oranges and golds bronzing us in its mellowing light.

"I've seen the way you look at him," she said, sipping from a delicate flute of Prosecco. Its tiny bubbles laced the sides of her glass. "And I don't blame you. He's gorgeous."

"It's that craggy rugged thing, it kills me."

"And—just saying—I've seen the way he looks at you too."

I'm not going to lie; not here, not now. I sat up straighter, even as I laughed, even as I tossed back the rest of my Prosecco. "Please," I said, perhaps a bit too loud. "Don't be ridiculous."

"This is your chance, Deena," she sing-songed, filling our glasses. "I'm telling you, all you need is the opportunity, he'll do the rest. Frankly, I was thinking something was going to happen while we were fishing."

My heart struck my chest with its fist; my cheeks flushed, remembering my imagined moment, my shame. "We've had plenty of moments and he's never batted an eye. And not just today, either, there was the afternoon you all went scuba diving without me."

"Maybe he needs a push," Laura said. "Some guys are like that. Just a suggestion: a head on his shoulder, a squeeze of his arm—"

I laughed. "He would run to the other side of the boat. Or jump off. He'd rather drown I'm sure than—"

"Look, I'm only saying that it doesn't have to be a big deal. It might make you feel better, make your marriage better, crazy as that sounds. You might get what you need in some way—and I'm not just talking about sex—but without changing your feelings for Buzz. You still love him, right?" Her soft brown eyes were serious.

I nodded, a simple head-bob. But there's nothing simple about it. "It won't work. When we get back, once Teddy's gone, that'll be it." As I spoke the words aloud I knew them to be true. "A marriage ends when one person chooses freedom."

"Oh, honey." She patted my hand. "It depends on your definition of freedom. You know I'm not an advocate of adultery in general, but in limited scenarios—in certain circumstances—I think it might be beneficial. Help you to see yourself through someone else's eyes."

I thought of your eyes; your ice-blue hands-off eyes.

Now, at dinner, Laura shrugs, smiling. "Oh, it's this dress," she says. "I got it on sale at Saks. And it's so comfortable! It's like wearing a nightie."

You and Dave are talking about the afternoon's fishing—bragging, really—about who caught how many skipjack and how large they were, how *freaking huge, did you see how monumental?* I listen to your voice, its brash ring like metal hitting metal, and turn away, shuddering.

"You're cold," Laura says.

I sip my wine, feel its warmth slide down my throat. "Oh no, not at all."

And then the steward appears with platters of raw tuna, the skipjack that was caught earlier in the day—sliced thin and drizzled with ponzu and minced jalapenos, rolled with rice and avocado into sushi, diced and mixed with lime juice and wasabi—delicate and fresh and spectacular all at once.

We all exclaim at the beauty of the fish, the skill of the chef, the success of the afternoon's fishing adventure. Laura recounts how her arms ached while reeling in her catch; Dave calls for bottles of champagne to be opened. We toast the chef, insisting he join us for a glass and the Captain as well. We toast each other, our health, the children, even the fish. We begin to sample the tuna, crying out in ecstasy over its freshness, its texture, the intricate flavors.

"Oh, I can't believe we have to leave all of this!" Laura says. She takes a sip of champagne and then licks her lips. "One more year until the last of the kids are off to college, and we can do this all the time."

"Some of us have to work, my dear," Dave says, kissing her cheek. He puts his arm around her shoulder and pulls her in to kiss her on the mouth. "Okay?"

I watch as Laura smiles and touches his cheek. She turns to me. "Well, just you and I can go somewhere, a girl's trip. Buzz won't mind, will you, Buzz?"

You shake your head—your mouth is full—as you help yourself to another sushi roll. Your handsome jaw is working, your eyes fixed on your champagne as you lift it towards your mouth. "Of course not," you say finally, after you've swallowed. "You girls should go."

"I don't know—" I settle back in my chair.

"Oh, come on," Laura says. "You've paid your dues! Four boys for God's sake and one in law school. They're all going to be gone, living their own lives—I mean, they already are, right? It's not like Teddy's ever even home anymore, and even so he's just got one more year—"

"I know I know," I say, looking down. All of a sudden a breeze brushes my skin, a fingertip touch, and I shiver. Its spectral stroke makes my bones ache; I hug myself. The yawning shadow of vacant rooms; the hollow click of a closing door; the tidiness of made beds a bleeding gash in the chest.

Captain Dick steps over to our table from somewhere inside. "How is everything tonight? Anyone need anything?"

We all smile and complement the food and the wine and the stars and our lives. You give toast after toast, draining your glass at the conclusion of each, tilting your head back, licking your lips. Captain Dick stands erect; listening; smiling. Finally, he turns to me. "How's your foot? Feeling better?" His voice is an electric pulse. I shiver again.

"So much better," I say. "Thank you. I think I just have a little chill." I wrap my arms around myself. "Too much sun this afternoon I suppose." I refuse to look at Captain Dick. Instead, I look at Laura: her expertly dyed-blonde hair—did you know she goes all the way into the city to get her hair done?—her manicured nails shell-pink, her teeth arctic-white. We are the same, Laura and I, yet different. I lack her confidence, her cunning.

"You see," Laura says, waving her glass of wine in the air. "You *are* cold."

"Why don't you go get a sweater?" you ask.

There is a pause.

"I guess I will." I push back my chair, shaking my head, a small unhappy smile on my face. The bandages around my ankle and foot glow toothpaste-white against my tanned skin.

"Here." Captain Dick takes my arm. "Let me help you."

"I'll get it," Laura says. "You sit right there."

"I can do it," I say.

"I don't mind," Captain Dick offers. "You all stay where you are."

"Oh no—*please*—" you begin, standing so quickly that your chair is knocked backwards. "Let me go, I'll get it. Which one would you like? The white one?" You bend over so you are talking in my face, mocking. "Or a different one? It's the very *least* I can do, you stay right where you are and don't move, don't hurt yourself, that's right." You straighten and turn quickly—almost too quickly, don't think I didn't notice the stumble—and disappear below. We sit, in silence, staring uncomfortably at each other.

Captain Dick bends down to right your chair, which you have left on its back, its legs in the air as if it were an upturned turtle. He looks up at me and nods, just a slight tilt of his chin, of silent recognition. I resist the urge to look away. His eyes shine ocean-black at me, so deep so welcoming I want to swim there. I let his eyes warm me, bundle me up and keep me safe, if only for a moment.

Dave clears his throat. "So who wants more sushi?" He picks up a platter next to him. "Or the tartare? There's a lot left. Deena?"

Laura puts her hand on his elbow, as if to silence him.

And even though I've barely eaten, and despite the fact that tuna tartare is my single favorite dish, I decline. The thought of putting food in my mouth makes me ill.

Later, the four of us stand on the deck by the railing, gazing out past the harbor and the moorings toward the horizon. It is a black night. A light wind stirs the humid air. Clouds pass across the moon, obscuring it, as if it were a Halloween night, and bats might come swooping from the sky. Captain Dick has discreetly dissolved into the shadows of the yacht's sleek interior, and I can hear the muffled clatter of dishes as the steward clears the table.

I listen to the running commentary between the three of you about the weather and the schedule for tomorrow, murmuring intermittently my assent. No one mentions the earlier scene; we are professionals, aren't we? Without looking, I feel Dave shift: he pulls Laura in towards him so that her back presses against his front, his arms circling her waist. He rests his chin against her shoulder, whispering something to her.

"Don't even go there," she laughs, elbowing him. "I mean it."

And us? You and I stand side by side, not touching. We look out at the water. We watch the dark sky heave above us as the water whispers its response, below. And I know what you must be thinking, then as well as now. Poor, pathetic Deena. But that's when my ankle turns in its mule, sliding fast along the deck's slick surface, and I am falling, grasping at the guardrail, lurching towards Dave, who takes a step back and trips over Laura, and she steadies him. I am reaching into the darkness, towards the water when I feel a strong hand, the captain's, close on my wrist and I'm pulled, hard, to safety, wrapped in his arms.

But I am wrong. It is you. It is your hand; your arms.

A year has passed, and as I pack for our annual trip I remember lying in bed with you that last night. I thought of going home the following day, and of our enormous house echoing empty. I thought of the meals I would prepare, just for the three of us and sometimes just for myself. I thought of our boys, all men now, and their gaping absence of need for me. I thought of the minutes ticking; the hours.

Perhaps you're shocked by my confession. Somehow, I doubt it. Disgusted maybe. Annoyed. A mosquito buzzing, whining in your ear.

I tuck my peach-striped bathing suit into the luggage, nestling your swim trunks underneath. I picture our first day on the yacht. I will change into this bathing suit, with a light linen sundress over it. The material will swish against my bare calves as I climb the stairs to the deck. Outside, I will look up at the blue-domed sky, the sun glaring white. I will walk to the stern, the thickness of the air my comfort. I will hold onto the guardrail. I will feel the smooth chill of metal in my palms. Slowly I will lower myself into the water's silk. It will circle my waist, press against me, hugging me close.

I will be utterly alone, soothed by the expansive attention of infinitesimal droplets of water, clinging to me, wanting me, embracing me.

CAFFEINE NIGHTS

- Chapter 4 -

Shanda Bahles

Kat crawled out of bed in the pre-dawn darkness. She sat at the rough wooden slab that served as their eat/work/play table and began a genius loci scan of the island and its inhabitants. They were leaving with Joey in less than an hour, and she wanted to feel the island's unique spirit one last time.

"Tante?"

Andrij's voice startled her, but she kept her eyes closed and maintained her focus. She put a finger to her lips. A full scan of the island wasn't easy. There were only thirty-two full-time residents, but they were scattered over three hectares.

"I can help."

"What?" She snapped. Her eyes flew open. Now she would have to start over.

Her young cousin was standing in front of her, sleep tousled. He started to lift his palms and then dropped them. A fierce concentration settled on his face. At six years old, his features were still indistinct but carried a hint of the man he would become one day, and she saw Tomás there. In his thin face and wide mouth, eyes the color of jade, pale skin tanned the color of caramel. Reminders of her uncle that both saddened and touched her.

He gave up and raised his hands. "I show you."

She regretted having snapped at him and relented. Taking hold of his hands, she connected with Andrij through their bond. He placed an image of Hinano, his babysitter, in her mind. He wanted her to find Hinano.

She sighed. With daily practice, her inventory of souls on the island had gotten easier, but seeking out and finding a specific person was still difficult. He would miss Hinano and her three children, his playmates. She could do this for him. With Andrij's mind still powering the image, she reached out to search for Hinano.

In that instant, every soul on the island lit up in her consciousness. She knew exactly where everyone was, what they were doing, and how they felt about it: bored, angry, curious, surprised, anxious…. Without effort and without reaching out to touch anyone's mind, she just knew. She withdrew her attention back to Andrij and stared at him with her mouth open.

"Jesus, Andrij. I had no idea you could do that." She wasn't sure if the excitement she felt was her own or coming from Andrij. The shock was definitely hers.

He shook his head and shared an image of the two of them palms touching, eyes closed.

"You mean, it's the two of us doing it?"

He nodded his head vigorously up and down.

"Yes." His smile grew wider. "I can help. We can be stronger together."

She remembered Tomás's description of the Institute's development of pair-bonding. A bond developed specifically to create a conduit between two Talents so that the dominant Talent could amplify and strengthen his or her skills by tapping into the power of the other Talent, typically a younger and less powerful one. The Institute used it to increase the capabilities of its psy-agents.

A horror filled her. She slammed shut the bond between them, before the image that had conjured the horror could fully form. Children at the Institute who, pair-bonded to adults who used them to amplify their abilities, were broken, pushed beyond their limits. Their Talent damaged or destroyed. Minds left vacant, and their bodies discarded. She shuddered.

"No." Kat pushed back from the table and jumped up.

Andrij's face went blank as he reacted to being shoved out of her mind.

"You must never allow anyone, not even me, especially not me, to use your power to enhance their own. It could damage you beyond repair. Do you understand?" Her voice ramped until she almost yelled the question.

Andrij's eyes widened

She'd frightened him. Well, dammit, that was good. He needed to be frightened.

Her phone beeped. "C'mon. We're late. Joey'll be frantic."

She looked up from her phone to see Andrij's face relax into a skeptical expression, distracted from his hurt feelings by her unlikely claim. She knew Joey had smoked too much weed over the last thirty years running dive shops in the South Pacific to get frantic over anything, let alone a routine trip to Papeete. And so, Andrij knew. He might be six years old, but through their bond, his access to her emotional maturity, such as it was, had made him wise for a six-year-old.

With a shake of her head, she texted Joey. And with a last look around at the simple but comfortable room that had been their home for the last six months, she shrugged on her pack and turned to help Andrij with his. She got her thoughts under control and allowed their bond to open as she knelt in front of him to adjust the straps on his pack

"*Tante*, can we come back?"

"I don't know, *mon petit*. But you'll always carry the island," she tapped his chest, "in here."

His sadness came to her in a faint smell of ashes. She steeled herself against it. She didn't know how Matin Xancovich had found them. But now that he had, the island was no longer safe.

"Now, remember. It's very important Joey doesn't know you are with me. The more he knows, the more danger he is in."

"*Oui*."

"Good. Show me your shielding."

She waited until his eyes squeezed shut in concentration, relaxed and reopened. All expression left his face. She reached for his mind, sensing the smooth polished surface of his current favorite shield metaphor—a steel ball bearing, deflecting all incoming empathic signals and sealing off all out-going ones. He presented a blank, slippery surface.

People needed empathic signals to register each other's presence. By blocking those signals it was possible to be nearly invisible. She doubted even another Talent would notice a fully-shielded Andrij in a crowd. Joey would only notice Andrij if he bumped into him or if Andrij called out.

"Good. Now share with me our version of boarding the dive boat."

If Joey did notice him, Andrij, with Kat heightening his focus and signal strength would implant a false memory that removed Andrij from the scene.

She took Andrij's hands. She was transported to the dock, looking through Andrij's eyes at his alternative reality. One in which she alone boarded the dive boat.

His Talent still amazed her. She watched the scene unfold in her mind's eye. It had taken her some months to differentiate between images her own eyes processed and those that Andrij shared with her. In his, every line had a shadow. It was as if the images from Andrij's mind came with an infinitesimal delay. Objects acquired a slightly greater thickness, or density, like a pen and ink watercolor reimagined as an oil painting. She dropped his hands and the image faded.

"Once we are on the boat, you go below and hide. Okay? Joey mustn't know you are with me."

Andrij's face reanimated, and a whiff of confusion punctuated his question. "*Oui. Mais . . .*" He held his hands out in a plea.

"Words please."

"You will help me…"

She nodded her encouragement.

"Use my Talent."

She nodded again.

"To…to stay safe."

"Yes. Exactly."

"Why is it bad for me to help you?" The hurt he'd felt earlier when she shut him out and shouted at him played across his mobile features.

Reminded of the children abused by the Institute, she'd been horrified at the thought of using him as a conduit. He didn't understand the risks. She did. That was why it was wrong for him to be a conduit but not wrong for her to be a conduit.

"Because I am able to give you permission to use my Talent. You cannot give me permission because you are too young."

The smell of wet wool underscored his obvious confusion. She doubled down.

"And because you are too young, it's hard for you to understand."

His confusion hardened to stubbornness. She recognized that stony smell all too well. He hated to be told he was too young. She couldn't imagine what he would be like as a teenager. She could only hope she had taught him well enough by then.

"Enough questions for now. We need to leave. Joey will leave without us."

With an eye-roll worthy of a teenager, Andrij exhaled.

She tousled his hair and tugged on his straps one more time. "You're right. But let's go."

Kat drew her first easy breath once they were underway, Andrij safely hidden beneath a pile of life jackets in the aft cabin. Joey was at the helm. The Aussie dive shop owner was younger than his grizzled appearance suggested. His skin, baked gingersnap cookie crisp by three decades of South Pacific sun, was covered with snow-white fuzz on his chest and arms. His 'boy-band' hair gone more salt than pepper.

Once past the coral reef that protected the atoll, Joey gunned it. The boat, freed from the weight of tourists and dive gear, flew through flat water. With minimal caffeine in her system, all of Kat's senses vied for primacy. The motor thrumming through the soles of her bare feet, the roaring of the engine cocooning her, the wind pulling at her clothes. Every kilometer they sped away from Petit Ta'a, her shoulders dropped another millimeter with the feel of the sun on her face, the taste of salt spray on her tongue, and Joey's happiness filling her nose with the leesy smell of champagne.

"Cap'n Joey to Sofia. Come in, Sofia. Over." Joey was yelling over the engine noise and waving at her. Thrown out of paradise, it took her a moment to remember she and Andrij were now Sofia and Andy.

"Sorry." She moved forward into the area semi-protected by

a tattered dodger. Without paying guests to worry about, Joey had stowed the bimini top to save on wear and tear.

"You look about a hundo feet down and nitro narc'd."

She shook her head. "I'm just enjoying being out on the water without a million things to look after."

"You mean without a dozen assholes to keep happy."

"That too." They grinned at each other. She wished she could tell Joey how nice he smelled. How his emotions generated a bouquet that reminded her of home. Of the Sausalito marina where her father's boat still swayed in its berth. How his years of daily pot smoking gave him an emotional profile that reminded her of Naked Pete, her favorite marina resident and former babysitter whose decades long daily morning yoga practice provided his bliss.

Until last year when he was murdered. Her smile faded.

"Whatcha got going in Papeete?"

Color rose in Kat's face. She was grateful for the wind and spray. She didn't lie often. Since she always knew when others were lying, she couldn't avoid feeling they knew when she was. Andrij nuzzled her mind. Even with their bond closed, they remained aware of each other. He had sensed her sudden discomfort. She reassured him all was well before giving Joey her prepared answer.

"Just a bit of tiny island fever. I suddenly realized I couldn't go another four weeks without a haircut, a mani-pedi and other girl stuff that won't cost me my entire month's salary. I've got a full day of personal maintenance planned. How 'bout you?" She pushed a bit of uncomplicated anticipation at him.

"Awesome." Joey's eyes twinkled with his anticipated pleasures. "I've got a pretty full day myself. Let's meet up at Marti's Roti for dinner. We'll head back after we fuel up on some of her ghost pepper jerk."

Mission accomplished.

The truth was she had booked the eleven a.m. flight to Auckland for her and Andrij. One-way. With any luck, they would reach New Zealand before Joey realized that she wasn't coming back. She had a note prepared for him. An apology, thanks, cover story all rolled into one.

If anyone came looking for her, he would say he gave her a ride. He wouldn't say anything about a small boy, because no one would ask. It was risky, he might mention 'Andy' in passing, not knowing how important it was for Andrij not to exist. Because it was infinitely less likely that someone believed to be dead would be found.

But it was less risky than asking him to stay quiet, leaving that knowledge in his mind to be plucked out by someone who knew how. She had considered briefly blurring his memories of Andrij, encouraging them to fade until Joey remembered only a young boy, maybe it was a girl, ten years old or so, who stayed on the island for a while with his/her mother. But she couldn't muddle the brain of everyone on the island. Too much to manage. Not even considering the moral implications.

The bigger issue was that she would have to draw on Andrij's Talent to do it. And she was convinced that was a step onto a dark path, one too dangerous to risk.

"I'll see how my day goes. If not, I'll meet you at the boat by nine p.m."

She leaned back and scanned the horizon. The sky was an unbroken blue. The only white, a few contrails crisscrossing miles high in the upper atmosphere. There was scarcely any wind, and the surface of the ocean was glassy. Long, low swells rolled unbroken all the way from Fiji until they hit the main island of Tahiti. They created a subsonic beat that would, if you let it, slow heart and respiration to a state that soothed the soul. The cinder cone of Bora Bora rose majestically from the flat sea, green and purple defiance in the misty north. Today it was clear of the wreath of clouds that were usually tethered to its peak.

She shifted her gaze back to Petit Ta'a and Ta'a, the larger island rising behind its namesake. A glint of sunlight on the water caught her attention. She reached out with her mind, but it was too far. Andrij, aware of her shifts in attention, made his willingness to help known. She gently but firmly shut him down. Joey's companionable ramblings faded into the background as she focused her attention on the sparkle. She watched with growing alarm as it became clear it was a boat heading in their direction.

"Hey Joey." She interrupted him mid-sentence, salivating over how Marta grew and dried her own ghost peppers for her famous jerk sauce. "You know anyone else planning to leave the island early today?" Sunday was change-over day. Arrivals were slotted for late afternoon, and departing guests usually waited until the last possible moment to leave their semi-private island paradise.

"Nope."

"Fast boat coming our way."

Joey turned and squinted. "Grab the wheel." Without waiting for her to move, he left the helm and dropped down the companionway. His tone was chill, but an adrenaline spike left the acrid smell of eucalyptus in his wake. Joey returned and trained his binoculars on the horizon.

"Merde, mierda, scheisse . . ." Joey was fluent in a dozen or more languages as long as he stuck to swear words. He dropped back into the cabin. She could hear him rummaging through the chart table, the ice box, and with another explosion of curses tore through his travel duffle. An alert Andrij popped into her head. She helped him stay hidden as Joey came up on deck with a handful of paraphernalia and a half-full plastic bag of cannabis. He opened the baggie, placed it around his nose and mouth and inhaled deeply before stuffing a handful into his mouth. Chewing like a cow on its cud, he offered her the baggie.

"Take the edge off? It takes about sixty minutes to kick in. We should be done with the flics by then."

Stunned by the lightning change in his demeanor, Kat stammered, "What?"

"It's the Frenchy's fast boat. The locals don't have any of those. Sure looks like it's heading our way. Can't take a chance. These fuckers don't mess around. The least worst thing they'll do is take my boat. And if I'm wrong, I've just tossed some very fine weed and my second favorite pipe. S'all good."

He extended the baggie again. She shook her head, and he grabbed another mouthful before taking a weight from the lead drawer and putting it in the baggie along with his pipe and papers.

126

He squeezed the air out, zipped it shut, and literally kissed it goodbye with a loud smack before tossing into their wake.

Taking up the binoculars, he watched for a while before saying. "Yeah. They're on an intercept. Slow it down a bit. No need to pound our kidneys just to put off the inevitable.

"Any chance of beating them to Papeete?" Kat still had the throttle at full speed.

"Nope. They're way too fast. Besides, no reason to now, the boat's clean." Joey stretched out at the stern with his feet up, his hat pulled low and his eyes closed. "Slow down and put her on auto-pilot."

Kat went below and told Andrij to hide. She settled him into a cupboard in the aft cabin where he seemed content to play at hide and seek. She returned to the cockpit just as the French police boat roared up, rocking Joey's boat with its enormous bow wave. An amplified voice demanded an invitation to board.

Joey came forward and cut the engine. The speedboat came alongside and settled into the water with a sigh. Joey moved a fender into place, and a young officer jumped across with a rope and tied the boats together.

"Claude, you old *putain*. What's got you out of bed so early on Sunday? Marianne throw you out again?" Joey greeted the captain with a grin so large and sincere that Kat thought the weed must be kicking in early.

The portly officer moved more easily between the boats than his girth would indicate and replied with a grin of his own.

"*Connard*. If not for you, I'd be there now, between her warm…" He stopped as if just noticing Kat standing at the helm. "*Désolé, je vous prie pardon, mademoiselle. A vôtre service.*" He made a slight bow and turned back to Joey. "M. Joey, I am afraid that we have a tedious business to attend."

Kat ignored the captain's facade. His relaxed, slightly apologetic demeanor belied a tense, defensive interior.

"There has been a theft from one of the guests at the resort. We are questioning everyone, of course. Naturally when you left so early this morning, we felt it necessary to speak with you." He turned to her, "and with Mademoiselle."

Kate smiled brightly at him while she reached into his mind. She found nothing to indicate he was in Xancovich's pocket. What tale had X spun that would justify forcing her to return to Petit Ta'a?

"Of course, *Monsieur.* Your job is not an easy one." With a dexterity that surprised even her, she teased out his warm feelings for Joey—currently dominated by his love of authority—and amplified them to counter his desire to complete his police work. And she had him. He relaxed under her persuasion.

"*Bien sûr.* We will do our search and get you back on your way." He gestured to the younger officer, "*Vite. Vite.* Take a look below." Before returning his attention to Joey, happy that the formalities would be observed.

As the young man moved with a determined step toward the companionway, Kat realized she had underestimated his independence. He was determined to do the job his captain was too old and fat to care about. His single-minded focus dominated his empathic output, and Kat had trouble finding an opposing thread to moderate his zeal. In a panic, she pretended to be knocked off balance by the movement of the boats pulling on each other and fell into his path. The officer stumbled, and she used that moment of distraction to reach into his mind, ensuring Andrij would have access.

"*Désolé, Capitan.* My apologies."

"*Non, c'est Lieutenant.*" He reddened but moved quickly past her into the main cabin.

Kat opened her bond with Andrij. He already had an image in his mind of the bulkhead covering over the cupboard. Acting as his conduit, Kat let the image move through her, sustaining and strengthening his effort by keeping the image in focus. She stood in the companionway so she could watch the young officer search. He rifled through Joey's duffel bag and opened every cupboard but the one he could not see.

Andrij remained safe, hidden in the aft cabin behind the veil he so effortlessly constructed and that she sustained.

The lieutenant returned to the deck with a quick shake of his head to his captain, and Kat drew her first easy breath since seeing the police boat leave Petit Ta'a in pursuit of them. She shared her relief with Andrij and thanks for a job well done before closing their bond. Her heart continued to pound as she said goodbye to the gendarmes.

MATISSE IN WINTER

- Part II, Chapter 3 -

Kristine Mietzner

Seattle, Washington. 1976

On a rainy Saturday morning in May, Camille woke to the sound of water lapping against the Edgewater Inn, a hotel built on pilings over Elliott Bay. She listened to the sea and watched Nick's chest rise and fall. She glanced at their image in the mirror. Her long blond locks fell on his freckled torso, heavily tanned from his travels to places sunnier than Seattle.

Naked and relaxed, she looked out the window at the Olympic Mountains. She imagined she was on a sailboat as she leaned into Nick's arms. When he stirred in his sleep, Camille kissed his ear. She admired Nick's firm muscles as he stretched. She arched her back when he stroked her hair. Camille traced the blood-soaked stitches on Nick's chest. "What happened?"

Nick leaned over to the nightstand, reached for his pack of Marlboros without answering her question, and pulled out a cigarette.

"I'd prefer you didn't smoke."

Nick lit his cigarette.

"Someone tried to kill me."

"Are you serious? Who?"

"Molly stabbed me."

"Your sister? What do you mean?"

"It was her disease, paranoid schizophrenia. The voices told her to do it."

"I had no idea." Camille brushed Nick's dark red hair from his face.

"She had bad luck with biology. But let's talk about you." He kissed Camille's neck. "Before I met you, I didn't know what I was missing."

"You didn't have me then, but now you do." Camille kissed his neck and then his ear. Her skin tingled when Nick drew her closer. She whispered, "I'd like to wake up next to you every morning."

"You really don't want to wake up with me every day."

She pushed him away. "How dare you say that? Why not?"

"You'd learn all my faults."

She doubted Nick had any serious faults. He'd been attentive and gentle for the past year. Camille questioned whether she'd been honest when she claimed she didn't want to get married. Until now, she'd planned to keep her childhood vow to stay single and childless. If he proposed, she believed she might break that promise.

That night, Camille inhaled Nick's familiar scent and pressed her breasts against his moist and warm chest. He spread his arms around her back and drew her closer. Camille loved the sensation of Nick's arms and legs wrapped around her and the rushing, melting, free-falling sensation of coming together.

On Sunday morning, as they ate breakfast at Pike Place Market, Nick said, "After I take you home, I'm going to see Molly."

"I'd like to visit Molly with you."

"She's too ill to have visitors, except close family." Nick took out his wallet and handed Camille a wad of folded bills. "Go shopping and enjoy yourself."

Camille gently pushed the money back into Nick's hands. "I appreciate the offer, but I don't want your money. I can buy my own clothes."

"I want to do things for you."

"You spend time with me. I enjoy being with you. That's enough."

"How about dinner?" said Nick. "Meet me at Shucker's Oyster Bar at the Olympic Hotel tonight at seven. There's something I want to talk about."

"See you then. I might have something to talk about also."

That night at Shucker's, a waiter carried a platter of oysters on crushed ice across the room to their table. When the tray lowered, the ruffled shells reminded her of a baby's baptism gown. An infant's cry from across the room made Camille jump.

When the waiter left, she whispered, "I have to tell you something."

"So, talk." Nick transferred the glistening morsels to two small plates. "You can't get oysters any fresher."

"My period is late."

He moved a plate toward Camille. "These were harvested in Willapa Bay this morning."

Did the hum of other customers' voices and the clattering of dishes drown her words out? Was he pretending not to hear, delaying, and buying time? "Did you hear what I said?"

Nick moved closer on the upholstered bench and spoke in a soft voice. "No, sorry. What's going on?"

Camille sat still and stared ahead. "My period is late."

Nick's eyes widened. He put down his oyster-filled fork. "How late?"

"Six weeks." Camille flinched saying the words aloud. Until this afternoon, she had held on to the hope that her period would return, trying to will her body into releasing its monthly flow. "I had a positive pregnancy test this afternoon. Three tests, actually. The first, the second, and the third time, the line on the stick turned blue."

"I thought you were taking the pill."

"I am. Something went wrong. I can't explain it. I took the pills every day. I didn't want this to happen." Nick was the only man in her life, the first one she had stayed with through an entire year; and now, they were beginning their second year together.

In a soft voice, Nick asked, "Do you think you might want to have a baby?"

Camille stared at him as tears suddenly spilled down her cheeks.

He wrapped an arm around her shoulder. "Okay. Okay." He took a napkin and dabbed Camille's cheeks. "I can help you in any way you want. Except, I don't see us getting married." Nick's voice had its usual warmth, but the words were cold.

"That's *not* helpful." She pressed her lips together and considered Nick's odd statement. He was willing to help her in any way, except by walking down the aisle. Her mind filled with a red rage that blocked her capacity to hear.

Nick, however, was saying something, and she needed to listen to whatever it was. She had to avoid shouting and acting out the same way her mother had always behaved under stress. There had to be a way to discuss the situation. Camille looked into his green eyes.

Nick squeezed her waist gently. "I'm surprised, that's all."

"If I wanted a child, you'd be my first choice as its father."

Camille yearned to hear Nick say he'd marry her and they would raise the child together, but his face went blank. He had lost his usual carefree expression. His next words stunned her. "You have another year of graduate school. You could have the baby during your last year, and then get a job teaching art history."

Camille forced herself to stay calm. "On the one hand,

you're suggesting I could carry this child. At the same time, you announce that you're not interested in marriage. I'm confused."

"Maybe I'm mixed-up, too. I might like having a baby."

"But not a wife?"

"I don't see myself marrying you." He looked away. "I'm sorry."

Camille's face burned as if she'd been slapped. "Sorry? I'm sorry, too." She touched the sleeve of Nick's tweed jacket and shook her head. "We've been dating for a year. I'm pregnant, and you don't see yourself getting married?"

Nick brushed her cheek with the back of his hand. "Whoa. From the day we met, you told me that you didn't want a husband. I took you at your word." He held her face in his hands and kissed her forehead. "It's not the end of the world. Remember Roe vs. Wade? You get to decide what you want to do."

"When I wasn't pregnant, it was easy to say I didn't want to get married. Now, I am. If I did have a baby..." she paused and then spoke slowly. "I would be a devoted mother and the wife of the baby's father." Camille scooted closer to Nick, placed her hand in his, and looked into his eyes.

Nick pulled Camille's chin toward him. "Listen. I'll help you in any way you want. Have the baby. Have an abortion. It's up to you. You decide. I love you, and I'll support your decision."

"Are you saying we would have the baby and be a family?"

"No, I'm saying I'll financially support you. But you would be a single mother. We would not be a family."

Camille's heart sank.

Nick pulled a paper from his breast pocket. "I'm scheduled

to fly to Los Angeles in the morning, and I get back on Tuesday evening. I'm going to give you the name of a doctor who can take care of your pregnancy, if that's what you want."

"How do you know the name of an abortion doctor?" Instantly she felt jealous over the idea of other women in Nick's life who might also have had abortions. She guessed she did not have Nick to herself but pushed away the thought.

"Over the years, more than one member of my flight crew has had unwanted pregnancies. Abortion is legal and more easily available in Seattle than some other places. I can't help hearing about it."

"Tell me more." Camille pressed her side against Nick's and focused on breathing evenly. "What's his name? Where's his office?"

"His name is Dr. Thayer. His office is near Sea-Tac. This is what you need to do. Look in the phone book or call information for his number."

Camille wrapped her arms across her waist, nodded, and turned to Nick.

"Get an appointment. Make it for Wednesday if he can fit you in. We'll go see him when I get back, if that's your choice."

Camille didn't know what she wanted. She folded her hands and rested them on her belly.

"I'll take care of you. Everything will be okay." He motioned to a passing waiter, who returned and refilled Nick's wine and Camille's ice tea. Nick raised his glass. "To you and your choice."

"I don't feel like I have much of a choice." She sipped the tea and took a deep breath. "I have to leave, Nick."

"We haven't finished dinner."

"I'll get a taxi. I need to think things over." She slid out of the booth and pulled on her coat.

"Let me take you home." He rose and stood beside her.

"No! I'll be fine. I need to be alone and think things over. Don't follow me."

"I'll call you."

Camille picked up her purse, walked through the restaurant, the hotel lobby, and into the cool Seattle night.

ABOUT THE AUTHORS

Maryam Soltani was born in a city by the Caspian Sea, and has lived in different parts of the world. For a while, she adopted Montreal as her home and attended McGill University, earning an undergraduate degree. Later, she moved to the United States and completed her graduate degree at Cambridge, Massachusetts. Maryam also completed a two-year novel-writing program at Stanford University and was selected to read a section of her novel at the Litquake Literary Festival in San Francisco. Currently, she calls Seattle home where she lives with her husband. Maryam enjoys brisk walks in the morning along with a shot of espresso. She also takes pleasure in spending time with her family and friends, meditating, practicing yoga, cooking, watching movies, skiing, swimming, paddle boarding and above all travelling.

Michael R. Hardesty is a lifelong resident of Louisville, KY, and is the author of two children's books and an Amazon Best Seller novel, *The Grace of the Ginkgo*. He holds a Baccalaureate degree in Commerce from the University of Louisville as well as a Certificate of Writing in Long Fiction from Stanford University's OWC Program. Hardesty's favorite pastimes are writing and hobnobbing with his three grandchildren.

Deborah Kevin (pronounced "key-vin") loves helping visionary entrepreneurs attract their ideal clients by tapping into and sharing their stories of healing and truth. She's a member of the Association of Writing Professionals, Association of Ghostwriters, and the National Association of Memoir Writers. A graduate of the State University of New York at Geneseo, Stanford University's Creative Writing program, and a Penn State University alumnus, Ms. Kevin is a former online editor of *Little Patuxent Review*. Her passions include travel, cooking, hiking, and kayaking. She lives with her family in Maryland.

Suanne Schafer, born in West Texas at the height of the Cold War, finds it ironic that grade school drills for tornadoes and nuclear war were the same: hide beneath your desk and kiss your rear-end goodbye. Now a retired family-practice physician, her pioneer ancestors and world travels fuel her imagination. She planned to write romances, but either as a consequence of a series of failed relationships or a genetic distrust of happily-ever-after, her heroines are strong women who battle tough environments and intersect with men who might—or might not—love them. Suanne's debut women's fiction novel, *A Different Kind of Fire*, due out November 1, 2018, explores the life of a nineteenth century artist who escapes—and returns—to West Texas. Her next book, *Hunting the Devil*, due out in 2019, reveals the heartbreak and healing of an American physician caught up in the 1994 Rwandan genocide.

When not writing poetry and futurist fiction, John Maly is a legal consultant and an expert witness in patent cases. He's worked as a United States patent agent, a microprocessor hardware engineer, a Unix software engineer, and an inventor. Other glamorous postings include working as a retail droid, fixing broken PCs, and selling used golf balls. John lives in the Bermuda Triangle with his two amazing daughters and a fluffy puppy. Find him on Twitter: John_W_Maly.

Roy Dufrain is a reformed college dropout, chronic hitchhiker, street musician, dive-bar pool shark, speedfreak and newspaper-man. He now holds a B.A. in Liberal Studies from Sonoma State University and is a recent graduate of the Novel Writing Certificate program at Stanford University. His fiction and non-fiction have appeared in *Scarlet Leaf Review*, *Noyo River Review* and *Coachella Review*. He lives in the hills of Northern California with a wife and a mortgage, and makes a living as the editor and publisher of a travel magazine for visitors to the Mendocino Coast.

Kenton K. Yee completed the OWC in 2014. His mentor was Val Brelinski. Since then, he has continued to study on his own, publishing occasionally in venues like *Daily Science Fiction* and *Strange Horizons*. He may or may not be in a whorl.

Diane Byington was in the first OWC class. She has been a tenured college professor, yoga teacher, psychotherapist, and executive coach. Also, she raised goats for fiber and once took a job cooking hot dogs for a NASCAR event. She still enjoys spinning and weaving, but she hasn't eaten a hot dog or watched a car race since. Diane's first novel, *Who She Is*, was published by Red Adept Publishing in March, 2018. She and her husband divide their time between Boulder, Colorado, and the small Central Florida town they discovered while researching her novel. Diane likes to write about offbeat people and experiences. Her work in progress is about an astronaut who joins a cult.

Victoria Grant is a baby boomer, born nine months after the end of World War II; raised within the social confines of the Betty Crocker fifties; broke those chains in the Age of Aquarius freedom of the sixties; matured under the fragile shelter of the not-quite-fulfilled female empowerment and racial equality promise of the seventies; nearly starved during the It's-All-About-Me eighties while teaching herself computing, then thrived in the tech-boom nineties. A native-born New Yorker born to native-born New Yorkers, she's also lived her adult life in the Southeast, Southwest, and on a Caribbean island. Writing— fictional adventures, observations, and experiences—has been a calling since childhood, and she's currently applying final touches to her debut novel.

Shanda Bahles is on her third career, second dog and first husband. After stints in technology startups and venture capital, she returned to her first love, writing. In her novels, the world is a better place. The women are strong, the men 'woke,' and the good guys win—eventually. Shanda lives in Menlo Park with the aforementioned great husband. They have two amazing children and one terrific dog.

Raised in the Pacific Northwest, Kristine Mietzner attended the University of Washington and then worked as a broadcast journalist in Alaska. Later, she taught school in California, including a year of full-time teaching at a state prison. Currently Kristine works for the California Department of Veterans Affairs and serves as a volunteer instructor of the Women Veterans Writing Workshop in Sacramento. Her writing has appeared in *Your Life is a Trip*, several California newspapers, and the anthology *Something that Matters, Life, Love, and Unexpected Adventures in the Middle of the Journey*. *Matisse in Winter* was workshopped in the Stanford Novel Writing Certificate Program and was a finalist in the San Francisco Writing Conference Writing Contest. Kristine lives in northern California with Max, her non-literary but loyal golden retriever.

Made in the USA
San Bernardino, CA
05 December 2018